A Monsoon Feast

A Monsoon Feast

Verena Tay (Editor)

monsoon

monsoonbooks

First published in 2012
by Monsoon Books Ltd, UK

www.monsoonbooks.co.uk

ISBN (paperback): 978-981-4358-83-5
ISBN (ebook): 978-981-4358-84-2

Cover design©Cover Kitchen

Contents

Foreword

More than Stories: Ways to Knowing
by Kirpal Singh

I believe it was the tortured Muriel Rukeyser who stated that the universe was full of *stories*, not *atoms*. Embedded in her curious utterance are so many different layers, so many stories, each waiting to be culled. Readers are normally of two varieties: those who just want a read and those who want more than just a read. I am very happy that *A Monsoon Feast* will satisfy both varieties. For here are stories which one can *just read* but they are also stories which offer *more than just a read*. And this is the triumph of the collection – to succeed in offering us a rich store of narratives which engages and which clearly points us to see more.

Let's begin by reflecting on the opening sen tence of the story by my good, old friend, Christine Suchen Lim:

In one minute's time, the electric bell will bong!

Now, one could be fussy and say – since the story is, among other things, about schools and learning and teaching (things our author knows only too well having been in the good employ of the Education Ministry for decades!) – there is no real need for the word 'time' since 'In one minute' states the same point. Ah, well, does it? Should we be finicky, picky and bother/worry about such details? Or should we not? And what about that interesting word *bong*? Frankly, how many of us would have used such a word to describe the sound coming from a bell? And please do note it is an *electric* bell. When both Christine and I were in school we didn't hear electric bells; what we heard was the bell being held and rung by burly men and women keen on making sure we school kids were obeying the call of the bell! There is more: in writing that apparently simple first sentence, the writer cleverly traps us in a world which is going to reveal some terrible goings-on – from relationships to jealousies, envies and allusions to high hopes and big reputations. Of course, the author is an old hand at telling stories – as they all are in *A Monsoon Feast*.

These days it is almost common to pick up anthologies of stories which pertain to a theme or a fixed style – or, more scintillatingly, attempt to seduce us by proffering sensational reality-checks very thinly disguised as fiction. It is a pleasure to realize that the current collection suffers from none of these. Though comprising only a few stories, *A Monsoon Feast* invites us to read, ponder, reflect, engage, respond. Is it therefore an anthology with an agenda? Yes. But the agenda is the old, familiar and noble one of transporting us, even briefly, to worlds, which while striking us as being so familiar, so readily recognizable, are also worlds which displace and plunge us into thoughts and arouse emotions which are best experienced perhaps privately in the comforts of our own reading spaces. Allow me to cite here the very disturbing story by Felix Cheong, *Because I Tell*:

> Cheche takes me to the bedroom and closes the door. She says, 'Why do you have to tell Mama? See what you did?' I say I forget it is a secret. Cheche says, 'You always forget. You were born stupid. You will always be stupid.'
>
> I say I am not stupid. I keep secrets. I never tell Mama Cheche takes Terence one time to her bedroom. I never tell Mama Terence kisses Cheche and holds her on the bed. I never tell Mama Terence tickles Cheche and they wear no clothes and they laugh loud. Cheche hits my face. She goes out of the house but forgets to take her keys. I cry and I put a pillow on my pain. Too many, many secrets to forget!

Just this small glimpse into the world of the poor child who is subjected to know but keep 'secrets' frightens because of the implicit immorality of what he experiences. The ironic stretch of dramatization here, exploiting deftly our own inner knowledge and our constant struggle to 'keep secrets' challenges a more-than-normal state of personal and familial morality. What do we as adults, grown men and women with

11

responsibilities and good jobs and reputations to uphold, inflict on our young? And why do we expect our young, those in our charge, to not tell when we preach honesty is the best policy? Or don't we? The story is a powerful reminder of the pitfalls of easy moralization, of the terrible dangers which lurk just beneath the veneer of social and personal respectability. Nothing we have not been told about by other writers. But Felix Cheong does it in a manner which is very close to home because so many of us know this is the hard, unaccepted truth.

Just like many other truths. So the remarkable story by Jaishree Misra – one of the finest in the collection – swiftly and almost with a casual air of nonchalance, betrays the broader hypocrisy which spreads to us all either because we become, willy-nilly, victims of our own making. How many of us, as we read this painful story of anguish and near betrayal, identify with its devastating *expose*? How many of us know the likes of Manichettan – this one-of-a-kind who is the life of every party, the hero on everyone's lips? How many of us, dare I ask, are Manichettans, not ever daring or wanting any one to discover our secret? Told with great subtlety, *A Life Elsewhere* captures that ever awesome question: where do we draw the line? Where do we stop in our quest for truth, Truth? The conclusion is worth quoting in full:

I ought to have been all puffed up that Manichettan had given me such a generous and trusting glimpse into his life, a far bigger deal than showing me his flat and giving me all the details of his job. Had he deliberately picked me of all the cousins to reveal this aspect to: his life in Singapore and this new kind of happiness he had found? But, as I turned to walk into the hotel lobby, it was a strange kind of fear that I felt, fluttering somewhere deep inside my stomach. Stepping into the lift, I thought of the number of times I had grandly predicted that Manichettan would die before making his parents unhappy. It was truly no exaggeration that he would far rather invite anguish on himself than see pain in his mother's eyes. That was just the kind of person he was. Did he now expect me to go back to our family in India and smooth his path for him in some way? I felt renewed panic; it was *he* who had always had that kind of clout with our elders, not me! I thought of how hard it would be to take up Manichettan's case, of the tears that would flow and the noisy recriminations that would follow. Would it be best to merely stay silent – as Manichettan himself had done all these years – so that he could cling to the happiness he had found for as long as he possibly could?

The narrative voice here appeals to us for sympathy, nay, empathy. Is this mere rationalization or the ultimate glory of the story-teller? Would it be best to stay silent? So many of us do; even smugly.

I return to Rukeyser's statement: the universe is full of

stories, not atoms. Yes, the atoms are there for sure – all the great scientists (Rutherford, Einstein) can't be wrong. But Rukeyser's is a quintessential observation – our stories are shrouded (note 'shrouded') in atomic silences and it is the writer's special gift to give these silences a voice. All the writers in *A Monsoon Feast* do this with alacrity. And the articulations present us with not only a delectable invitation but also, I should add, a vexing trial. These are not stories for the weak-minded or weak-hearted for they tax our capacities for fellow-feeling; a humane response getting rarer and rarer.

Kirpal Singh, noted poet, fictionist, critic, scholar, is currently with the Singapore Management University where he is Director of the Wee Kim Wee Centre.

Foreword

The Anxiety of Audience:
Reflections Prompted by *A Monsoon Feast*
by Shashi Tharoor

The stories in this collection reflect an unusual meeting of two streams of post-colonial literary writing in English, those of Kerala and Singapore. Prof Kirpal Singh has looked at them with a Singaporean scholar's eye; my perspective as a Malayali (as Keralites are called, since they speak Malayalam) is somewhat different. Though I am a Malayali and a writer, I am not a Malayali writer; my literary production has been entirely in English. That is true of the other Kerala writers represented in this volume. For us, the evocation of a Kerala sensibility occurs in a language other than that of the state's famous literary tradition. To write of and from Kerala, but not to do so in Malayalam, involves a choice that some would argue is also a distancing.

The Malayalam literary tradition goes all the way back

to the 16th century efforts of the legendary Thunchath Ezhuthachan, who first established Malayalam as a literary language. He was born at a very different time, in an era where knowledge was the monopoly of a few and the transmission of culture was confined to a handful of Brahmins – a community to which Thunchath Ezhuthachan did not belong. Despite being born into a socially underprivileged caste – the Chakala Nairs – whose members were forbidden to learn the Vedas, he defied the ossified traditions of his time and both gently and firmly thwarted the attempts by the entrenched interests of the day to keep him away from learning. Thunchath Ezhuthachan mastered the Vedas and the Upanishads without the support, let alone the blessings, of the upper castes. In this, he captured the spirit of determination that all Keralites are proud of – the determination to overcome all obstacles in the pursuit of education and the development of culture. The thriving literary culture of Kerala is a reflection of this proud tradition. Despite not having undergone comparable struggles, the English-language writers represented in this volume are heirs to this cultural and literary legacy.

But yes, they write in English. As a Malayali and a writer who is not a Malayali writer – and as a writer in English who is not English, but focuses very much on India – I am said to suffer from what one critic called 'the anxiety of audience'. Whenever I am asked (which is more often than I would wish) to address listeners or readers about my writing, I have to confess I approach the task with some diffidence. Writers are supposed to write; we should leave the pontificating to the critics. But once in a while even writers are forced to think about their craft. And I suspect that many of the writers from Kerala you will encounter in these pages have been asked the question I find myself constantly answering: 'Who do you write for?'

The assumption behind the question is that there is something artificial and un-Indian about an Indian writing in English. I write about India in a language mastered, if the last census is to be believed, by only 2 per cent of the Indian population. There is an unspoken accusation implicit in the question: am I not guilty of the terrible sin of inauthenticity, of writing about my country for foreigners?

This question has, for many years, bedevilled the work of the growing tribe of writers of what used to be called Indo-Anglian fiction and is now termed, more respectfully, Indian Writing in English. This is ironic, because few developments in world literature have been more remarkable than the emergence, over the last two decades, of a new generation of Indian writers in English. Beginning with Salman Rushdie's *Midnight's Children* in 1981, they have expanded the boundaries of their craft and of their nation's literary heritage, enriching English with the rhythms of ancient legends and the larger-than-life complexities of another civilization, while reinventing India in the confident cadences of English prose. Of the many unintended consequences of the Empire, it is hard to imagine one of greater value to both colonizers and colonized.

The new Indian writers dip into a deep well of memory and experience far removed from those of their fellow novelists in the English language. But whereas Americans, or Englishmen, or Australians have also set their fictions in distant lands, Indians write of India without exoticism, their insights undimmed by the dislocations of foreignness. And they do so in an English they have both learned and lived, an English of freshness and vigour, a language that is as natural to them as their quarrels at the school playground or the surreptitious notes they slipped each other in their classrooms.

Those who level the charge of inauthenticity (usually *in* English) base themselves on a notion of 'Indianness' that is highly suspect. Why should the rural peasant or the small-town schoolteacher be considered more quintessentially 'Indian' than the pun-dropping collegian or the Bombay socialite who is as much a part of the Indian reality? India is a vast and complex country; in Whitman's phrase, it contains multitudes. The world depicted in these stories is a very narrow slice of it, but it is Indian for all that. The critic M. K. Naik once suggested that the acid test ought to be: 'Could this have been written only by an Indian?' For most, though not all, of my stories, and certainly of my novels, I would answer that this could not only have been written only by an Indian, but only by an Indian *in English*. In that, and in the pleasure I hope the writing will impart, lies their principal vindication.

But this is not an English aimed at foreigners. Much of my own writing emerges from a sensibility comparable to the writers in this volume: with one or two exceptions the concerns, assumptions, and language of my fiction all emerge from the consciousness of an urban Indian male who has grown up in metropolitan India. I write for anyone who will read me, but first of all for Indians like myself, Indians who have grown up speaking, writing, playing, wooing and quarrelling in English, all over India. (No writer really chooses a language: the circumstances of his upbringing ensure that the language chooses him.) Members of this class have entered the groves of academe and condemned themselves in terms of bitter self-reproach: one Indian scholar, Harish Trivedi, has asserted (in English) that Indian writers in that language are 'cut off from the experiential mainstream, and from that common cultural matrix ... shared with writers of all other Indian languages.' Trivedi metaphorically cites the fictional English-medium school in a R. K. Narayan story whose students must first rub off the sandalwood-paste caste-marks from their foreheads before they enter its portals: 'For this golden gate is only for the *déraciné* to pass through, for those who have erased their antecedents.'

It's an evocative image, even though I thought the secular Indian state was *supposed* to encourage the erasure of casteism from the classroom. But the more important point is that writers like myself do share a 'common cultural matrix', albeit one devoid of helpfully identifying caste-marks. It is one that consists of an urban upbringing and a pan-national outlook on the Indian reality. I do not think this is any less authentically 'Indian' than the worldviews of writers in other Indian languages. Why should the rural peasant or the small-town schoolteacher with his sandalwood-smeared forehead be considered more quintessentially Indian than the punning collegian or the Bombay socialite, who are as much a part of the Indian reality?

I write of an India of multiple truths and multiple realities, an India that is greater than the sum of its parts. English expresses that diversity better than any Indian language precisely because it is not rooted in any one region of my vast country. At the same time, as an Indian, I remain conscious of, and connected to, my pre-urban and non-Anglophone antecedents: my novels reflect an intellectual heritage that embraces the ancient epic the Mahabharata, the Kerala folk dance called the *ottamthullal* (of which my father was a gifted practitioner) and the Hindi B-movies of 'Bollywood', as well as Shakespeare, Wodehouse and the Beatles.

As a first-generation urbanite myself, I keep returning to the Kerala villages of my parents, in my life as in my writing. Yet I have grown up in Bombay, Calcutta and Delhi, Indian cities a thousand miles apart from each other; the mother of my children is half-Kashmiri, half-Bengali; and my own mother now lives in the Southern town of Kochi. This may be a wider cultural matrix than the good Dr Trivedi imagined, but it draws from a rather broad range of *Indian* experience. And English is the language that brings those various threads of my India together, the language in which my former wife could speak to her mother-in-law, the language that enables a Kashmiri to function in Kochi, the language that serves to express the complexity of that polyphonous Indian experience better than any other language I know.

What is the Kerala tradition these writers draw from? Hailing from a land of forty-four rivers and innumerable lakes, with 1500 kilometres of 'backwaters', the Keralite bathes twice a day and dresses immaculately in white or cream. But she also lives in a world of colour: from the gold border on her off-white *mundu* and the red of her bodice to the burnished sheen of the brass lamp in her hand whose flame glints against the shine of her jewellery, the golden *kodakaddakan* glittering at her ear. Kerala's women are usually simple and unadorned. But they float on a riot of colour: the voluptuous green of the lush Kerala foliage, the rich red of the fecund earth, the brilliant blue of the life-giving waters, the shimmering gold of the beaches and riverbanks.

Yet there is much more to the Kerala experience than its natural beauty. Since my first sojourn as a child in my ancestral village, I have seen remarkable transformations in Kerala society, with land reform, free and universal education and dramatic changes in caste relations.

It is not often that an American reference seems even

mildly appropriate to an Indian case, but a recent study established some astonishing parallels between the United States and the state of Kerala. The life expectancy of a male American is 72, that of a male Keralite 70. The literacy rate in the United States is 95 per cent; in Kerala it is 96 per cent. The birth rate in the US is 16 per thousand; in Kerala it is 18 per thousand, but it is falling faster. The gender ratio in the United States is 1050 females to 1000 males; in Kerala it is 1040 to 1000, and that in a country where neglect of female children has dropped the Indian national ratio to 930 women for 1000 men. Death rates are also comparable, as are the number of hospital beds per 100,000 population. The major difference is that the annual per capita income in the US is about seventy times as much as that in Kerala.

Kerala has, in short, all the demographic indicators commonly associated with 'developed' countries, at a small fraction of the cost. Its success is a reflection of what, in my book *India: From Midnight to the Millennium*, I have called the 'Malayali miracle': a state that has practised openness and tolerance from time immemorial; which has made religious and ethnic diversity a part of its daily life rather than a source of division; which has overcome caste discrimination and class oppression through education, land reforms, and political democracy; which has given its working men and women greater rights and a higher minimum wage than anywhere else in India; and which has honoured its women and enabled them to lead productive, fulfilling and empowered lives.

More important, Kerala is a microcosm of every religion known to the country; its population is divided into almost equal fourths of Christians, Muslims, caste Hindus and Scheduled Castes (the former 'Untouchables', now called Dalits), each of whom is economically and politically powerful. Kerala's outcasts – one group of whom, the Pariahs, gave the English language a term for their collective condition – suffered discrimination every bit as vicious and iniquitous as in the rest of India, but overcame their plight far more successfully than their countrymen elsewhere. A combination of enlightened rule by far-thinking Maharajahs, progressive reform movements within the Hindu tradition (especially that of the remarkable Ezhava sage Sree Narayana Guru), and changes wrought by a series of left-dominated legislatures since Independence have given Kerala's Scheduled Castes a place in society that other Dalits across India are still denied. It is no accident that the first Dalit to become President of India is Kerala's K. R. Narayanan – who was born in a thatched hut with no running water, who as a young man suffered the indignities and oppression that were the lot of his people, but who seized on the opportunities that Kerala provided him to rise above them and ascend, through a brilliant diplomatic and governmental career, to the highest office in the land.

Part of the secret of Kerala is its openness to the external influences – Arab, Roman, Chinese, British, Islamist, Christian, Marxist – that have gone into the making of the

Malayali people. More than two millennia ago Keralites had trade relations not just with other parts of India but with the Arab world, the Phoenicians, and the Roman Empire. From those days on, Malayalis have had an open and welcoming attitude to the rest of humanity. Jews fleeing Roman persecution found refuge in Kerala; it is said they came to Kerala following the destruction of the temple of Judea by the Babylonians before the birth of Christ, and there is evidence of their settlement in Cranganore in AD 68, this time after Roman attacks. Later, fleeing the Portuguese, the Jews settled in Cochin 1500 years later, where they built a magnificent synagogue that still stands. (It is instructive that the Jews knew no hostility, let alone persecution, in Kerala until the Portuguese came from Europe to persecute them.) The Christians of Kerala belong to the oldest Christian community in the world outside Palestine, converted by Jesus' disciple Saint Thomas (the 'Doubting Thomas' of Biblical legend), one of the twelve apostles, who came to the state in AD 52 and, so legend has it, was welcomed on land by a flute-playing Jewish girl. So Kerala's Christian traditions are much older than those of Europe – and when St Thomas brought Christianity to Kerala, he made converts amongst the high-born elite, the Namboodiri Brahmins. Islam came to Kerala not by the sword, as it was to do elsewhere in India, but through traders, travellers and missionaries, who brought its message of equality and brotherhood to the coastal people. Not only was the new faith peacefully embraced, but it found encouragement in attitudes and episodes without parallel elsewhere in the non-Islamic world: in one example, the all-powerful Zamorin of Calicut asked each fisherman's family in his domain to bring up one son as a Muslim, for service in his Muslim-run navy, commanded by sailors of Arab descent, the Kunjali Maraicars.

It was probably a Malayali seaman, one of many who routinely plied the Arabian Sea between Kerala and East Africa, who piloted Vasco da Gama, the Portuguese explorer and trader, to Calicut in 1496. (Da Gama, typically, was welcomed by the Zamorin, but when he tried to pass trinkets off as valuables, he was thrown in prison for a while. Malayalis are open and hospitable to a fault, but they are not easily fooled.)

In turn, Malayalees brought their questing spirit to the world. The great Advaita philosopher, Shankaracharya, was a Malayali who travelled throughout the length and breadth of India on foot in the 8th century A.D., laying the foundations for a reformed and revived Hinduism. To this day, there is a temple in the Himalayas whose priests are Namboodiris from Kerala.

Keralites never suffered from inhibitions about travel; an old joke suggests that so many Keralite typists flocked to stenographic work in Bombay, Calcutta and Delhi that 'Remington' became the name of a new Malayali sub-caste. In the nation's capital, the wags said that you couldn't throw a stone in the Central Secretariat without injuring a

Keralite bureaucrat. Nor was there, in the Kerala tradition, any prohibition on venturing abroad, none of the ritual defilement associated in parts of North India with 'crossing the black water'. It was no accident that Keralites were the first, and the most, to take advantage of the post-oil-shock employment boom in the Arab Gulf countries; at one point in the 1980s, the largest single ethnic group in the Gulf sheikhdom of Bahrain was reported to be not Bahrainis but Keralites. The willingness of Keralites to go anywhere to do anything remains legendary. 'When Neil Armstrong landed on the moon in 1969,' my father's friends laughed, 'he discovered a Malayali already there, offering him tea.'

But Keralites are not merely intrepid travellers. Kerala took from others, everything from Roman ports to Chinese fishing-nets, and gave to the rest of India everything from martial arts (some of which appear to have inspired the better-known disciplines of the Far East) to its systems of classical dance-theatre (notably Kathakali, Mohiniattam, and the less well-known Koodiyattom, recently hailed by UNESCO as a 'masterpiece of the oral and intangible heritage of humanity'). And I have not even mentioned Keralite cuisine and traditional medicine, in particular the attractions of Ayurveda, the great health system of ancient India, with its herbs, oils, massages and other therapies, now revived and attractively presented at dozens of locations around our state. Why should none of this lend itself to expression in English?

Of course, there is no shame in acknowledging that

English is a legacy of the colonial connection, but one no less useful and valid than the railways, the telegraphs or the law courts that were also left behind by the British. Historically, English helped us find our Indian voice: that great Indian nationalist Jawaharlal Nehru wrote his *The Discovery of India* in English. But the eclipse of that dreadful phrase 'the Indo-Anglian novel' has occurred precisely because Indian writers have evolved well beyond the British connection to their native land. The days when Indians wrote novels in English either to flatter or rail against their colonial masters are well behind us. Now we have Indians in India writing as naturally about themselves in English as Australians or South Africans do, and their tribe has been supplemented by India's rich diaspora in the United States, which has already produced a distinctive crop of impressive novelists, with Pulitzer Prizes and National Book Awards to their names. Their addresses don't matter, because writers really live inside their heads and on the page, and geography is merely a circumstance. They write secure of themselves in their heritage of diversity, and they write free of the anxiety of audience, for theirs are narratives that appeal as easily to Americans as to Indians – and indeed to readers irrespective of ethnicity.

Surely that's the whole point about literature – that for a body of fiction to constitute a literature it must rise above its origins, its setting, even its language, to render accessible to a reader anywhere some insight into the human condition. Read my books and those of other Indian writers not because we're

Indian, not necessarily because you are interested in India, but because they are worth reading in and of themselves. And each time you pick up one of my books, ask not for whom I write: I write for you.

So – to go back to the collection you now hold in your hands – do the Kerala stories in this volume speak authentically of a Kerala experience? Yes, they do, even though they do not do so in Malayalam, the language of Kerala. Inevitably the English language fundamentally affects the content of each Kerala author's story, but it determines neither the audience of the writer nor the perception of the reader; language is, after all, a vehicle, not a destination.

Travel on this fine vehicle between Kerala and Singapore, and enjoy *A Monsoon Feast*.

An elected Member of Parliament, former Minister of State for External Affairs and former Under-Secretary-General of the United Nations, Shashi Tharoor is the prize-winning author of twelve books.

Big Wall Newspaper

Suchen Christine Lim

{ Dedicated to Lim Chi Minh }

In one minute's time, the electric bell will bong. The hungry horde will rush down the stairs and out through the school gates. But I'll be here, waiting for the Sengkang Kid. Thanks to the Auntie brigade this loo is clean and dry. That's how it is in our elite Saints' schools. We take pride in having a clean loo. And that's why the loo is the best place to have a fight. There's a clear space between the sinks and the urinals; and no teacher comes into the boys' loo. This block is deserted after school. There will be no spectators this evening. No smart-ass loudmouths to cheer him. It will be a clean fight between the Sengkang Kid and me. Not that I want to fight him. I don't like to fight. But that Kid tore up my Big Wall Newspaper.

I had written about the fight that the Kid lost after the soccer game last week. That got him so pissed he sent a fist towards my face, but I ducked. And all that punch and weight fell hard onto the floor. That got him madder. He swore to kick the hell out of my smart-ass face. This morning, he tore down our wall newspaper and showed it to the P.

Mr Harry Koh hit the roof when he saw the headline. Inside my pocket now is the P's note I've got to take home and show to my mom; my mom who pats her son on the shoulders each time he brings home a report card filled with A's and B's. These grades make her feel good. These grades make her feel her life is still worthwhile, and her divorce has not affected her boy. This note will make her cry tonight.

* * *

'You've got nothing better to do? So many other things happened in school. Why didn't you write about them?'

'This is news.'

That was his father's dictum: Dog bites man. Not news. Man bites dog. News. Of course, she understands why a young female teacher crying in front of her class is news in an all boys' school. But did he have to write about it and publish it in his Big Wall Newspaper, as he calls it?

'What happened in that Secondary Four class was none of your business! You didn't make this up, did you?'

'Mom!'

His eyes have that mix of fear and defiance that you see in a young dog when it's cornered. His tone is accusatory.

'You are the one who taught me to tell the truth.'

His face wears the look of a sullen mule. His voice is hoarse; it's changing fast. Soon he'll speak like a man. She wants to hug him and throttle him at the same time. Pride and annoyance surge through her. He's just fourteen and he's started a school newspaper. She reads his Principal's note again.

You are requested to attend an urgent meeting tomorrow at 8 a.m. sharp. Your son's abuse and violations of ... The note reels off a list of Wai Mun's offences: fighting, vandalism of the school's notice board, putting up notices without the Principal's permission, publishing a school newspaper without the Principal's permission, making a teacher cry. The punishment is a public caning. *Should his parents object, they are advised to take their son out of the school.*

Her hands are trembling a little, just a little. Her son is not a criminal. Her first impulse is to protect her boy. Her second is to seek 'damage control'. But what can she do? Vandals and errant students are caned in Singapore. But a public caning for a school boy? Even the most hardened vandal is caned in private in the prison. Not in front of an audience of a thousand students in the school hall! What will Richard say? For a fleeting second, she thinks of phoning him. But what's the point? He won't speak for his son. He can't even speak up for himself. O, God! What should she do?

'When did you start this stupid business?' she turns on the boy.

'Three weeks ago,' he growls.

'Haven't you anything better to do?' she screams at him.

'School's boring.'

'School's boring! So you fight and vandalise the school's notice board?'

'I didn't fight, Mom! That boy didn't turn up. I didn't vandalise the notice board! I pinned up *The Towgay News*.'

'What?' The surprise in her voice makes him smile.

'Rajiv said our Big Wall Newspaper should report bits of news about school. I said, ya, bits of news like bean sprouts. So we called it *Towgay News*.'

She wants to hug and slap him. The audacity of this boy. The pride in his voice is unmistakable. He brings out the offending newspaper – an A3-sized broadsheet with a green and yellow computer-printed masthead of bean sprouts, and the date, July 1989. Below the masthead are the names of the two reporters, and their editor, John Wong Wai Mun. She was the one who named him 'Wai Mun'. A Cantonese name meaning 'For the People'. She was young and idealistic then. She thought love could change the world.

Can it? Let's find out, Richard had whispered in her ear, his finger tracing the slight depression beneath her collarbone, sliding down the space between her breasts. She wants to scream at him now.

'Honestly, Mun! I don't know what to do with you. So tomorrow I've got to go and see the Principal about your vandalism.'

'I told you! It's not vandalism.'

'Don't you talk back to me like this! You're in deep shit already!'

'We only pinned up our newspaper on the board for everyone to read. We didn't want to print many copies. So we did one big wall newspaper. Like ... like the Chinese students in Tiananmen Square.'

'But you're not in China, Mun! You're in Singapore! In St Paul's! What's the matter with you?'

It's the top elite boys' school after Raffles' Institution (RI). 'We don't accept the rejects of RI. Is St Paul's your first choice?' That's how the Principal interrogates each poor sod who begs for a place for his son. Those whose sons are accepted will hear Harry Koh's sonorous voice booming through the loudspeakers. 'Parents! Give us your boys! We will return them to you as men! St Paul's results are exemplary. There are no failures in my school.'

'I'll have to take you out of that school.'

'No, Mom.'

'It's a public caning for God's sake! In the school hall! It's draconian and barbaric! You're only in Sec Two. You can start all over again in a new school.'

'No.'

She can't believe her ears, can't recognise this stubborn, mulish face in front of her. He looks just like Richard now. Just as stupid. Just as blind. The boy can't see that this is censorship of the worst kind. Not even the government would cane people for reporting a fact however unpalatable that fact. So. A young female teacher cried. So what? She's an adult and a professional who should be able to hold her own against a bunch of boys. Why should the school protect the adult against the child?

Her brain is ticking. She's marshalling all her arguments, lining them up against the school. Her boy and his friends had started a newspaper by themselves. A bunch of fourteen-year-olds. They should be applauded for their initiative. Not caned! *Forty pairs of male eyes stared in shock and wonder as tears rolled down Miss Tan's* ... Agreed! The report is a little sensational. The boys should apologise to the teacher, make amends, wash the school toilets, or pick up litter, or whatever! But not caned! Sensational reporting is not a crime punishable by caning. Starting a school newspaper without the Principal's permission is not a crime punishable by caning. What's the matter with this Principal? His school is not the state of Singapore. Does he think he's the Prime Minister?

She's raving and she knows it.

'I'll put you in a private school for now. Next year, I'll send you overseas.'

Her boy shakes his head.

'Why? Are you scared of leaving school?'

The boy stares resolutely at his feet, and refuses to answer her. His sulky silence infuriates her. She resists the temptation to shake him ... and hug him. She wants so much to protect him. But she knows he wants to be treated as a grown-up. Especially now that it's just the two of them in the family. But he's only fourteen. Oh, God! How can she let this stupid school destroy him?

'Mun, please,' she pleads.

He looks up, his eyes dark and accusing.

'You're the one who said we must accept the consequences of our action.'

*   *   *

My mom says school gives you an education. My mom is biased. She's a teacher. School is where you learn your life is over unless you mug and pass exams. School is where you learn to stand up and sing like a bloody idiot, 'Gooooood morrrrr-ning, teeeee-chur!' You find out at great cost to your dignity that you've got to take all the crap that grown-ups vomit out in front of your desk or else you fail. You learn not to challenge, not to argue with grown-ups. Unless. Unless you've a fatal attraction for insults or humiliation, or detention class, or standing outside the classroom until the grown-up is satisfied with your guard duty. School is where you learn power is in the hands of one man – the P. The P's office is a great place to feel small. You can't enter it unless his female dragons say 'Mr Koh will see you now.'

We're here in the P's office, my mom and I, and Seng and Rajiv's parents. Six chairs are arranged in a semi-circle in front of the P's table. The parents sit down. Five parents and a vacant chair. That must be for Dad. They don't know that my parents have split. We boys are told to stand behind our parents. I want to take away the empty chair next to Mom.

It's making her uncomfortable. Rajiv and Seng Huat's parents have come together. My mom is alone. I step forward. I stand between her and the vacant chair. This way, she can't see the chair. This way, she can see me standing beside her. She's not alone.

'Please wait.' The school clerk closes the door.

No one says a word. The parents sit like they're waiting for the funeral service to start. Mom is wearing her dark blue dress. Rajiv's mom is in a grey sari. Seng's mom wears a black pantsuit; and the two fathers are in dark trousers, long-sleeved white shirt and tie. This is how it is when the principal of your son's elite school tells you to come to his office. Rajiv, poor sod, looks like he's been bonked on his head. His father's face is grim. His back is ramrod straight, and his arms are folded in front of his chest. Not a good sign. Poor Rajiv's mom is staring at the floor. Seng Huat's fat face is the only one with a smile. But I know he's scared shit like Raj and me.

I watch the hands of the clock above Mr Koh's black leather armchair. Its *tick, tick, tick* is the only sound in the room. Then the door opens. Mr Koh enters. The parents stand up. They introduce themselves.

'Sit down. Please. Sit down. Sorry to keep you waiting. I had some urgent matters to attend to. Thank you for coming. Boys!'

'Yes, sir!'

'You know why your parents are here, don't you?'

'Yes, sir!'

'Vandalism is a serious offence …'

'Mr Koh, sorry, may I interrupt?'

That's my mom. She's not like other parents. She can't keep her gap shut.

'Yes, Mrs Wong.'

'Exactly what constitutes vandalism in St Paul's?'

'We have very strict rules governing the use of the school's notice boards in St Paul's. No teacher or student is allowed to put up anything without the Principal's prior permission. These boys broke that rule. They pinned up all sorts of papers without my knowledge and my permission. That constitutes vandalism. It's a serious violation. The school rules have been made known to all our boys from the day they joined this school. But these boys have flouted the rules.'

'Mr Koh, I agree that these boys have broken the school's rule regarding the use of the notice boards. But does this merit a public caning?'

'Mrs Wong, I cannot allow any Tom, Dick and Harry to pin up anything they wish without the Principal's expressed knowledge and permission. Such flagrant disregard of rules and regulations undermines the authority of the school and the principal. And I cannot allow it. This is a serious offence. And we cane boys for serious offences. Like smoking. They do harm to their own health. We cane them. These three boys have done harm not to themselves. Worse. They've done harm to a teacher's reputation and authority. They've destroyed my teacher's confidence. She's a young woman. New in the service. A scholar sent by the Ministry of Education. Now she wants to resign. Do you know how hard it is for me to retain teachers nowadays? A good teacher is hard to come by. Now if these boys had followed the rules, had come to me first, I wouldn't have let them publish this story. They should have gone to their teachers. Their teachers would've advised them. They would've vetted the boys' writing, corrected their mistakes, and sent them to see me in the office. But these boys went over their teachers' heads! Went over the principal's head! I'm the Principal of this school. I cannot let them go unpunished!'

'Mr Koh ...'

'Mrs Wong, I'm the Principal of this school. I set the rules. I'm in charge. When things go wrong, I'm responsible.'

He stares at Mom. I'm praying. I pray that Mom will keep her word. I place my hand on her shoulders to remind her of her promise. None of the other parents dare to say anything. Rajiv's father has unfolded his arms. His back is no longer ramrod straight. We watch in silence as Mr Koh opens the brown folder on his desk.

'If any of you wish to take your son out of my school, I will not stop you.'

Silence.

'Well then,' Mr Koh looks at us. 'If there's no objection to corporal punishment, please sign this document to give the school permission to cane your son. Rest assured. I will do the caning myself. Not the discipline master.'

*   *   *

That night, she can't sleep. She has failed her son. Where is her lively seven-year-old? Where's the little boy who had so bravely stood up for his friend in Primary Two? As an eight-year-old, her boy had refused to go for a class outing. *Because Miss Tan was unfair to Aziz, Mommy.* She was proud that he had insisted on staying back in school with his friend. At ten, he had written a note (with her help) to tell his class teacher why he and his friends hated Chinese. *Zhen Lao-shi brings a cane to class.* When did her boy change? How did the courageous little fellow turn into this compliant, silent teenager who accepts a public caning? Has she been so absorbed in her own despair that she has failed to notice his change? Has he become like his father?

Last night, she looked through the three issues of his Big Wall Newspaper again. Full of typical schoolboy humour, but the reports were well written. There were no grammatical errors. The boy had edited the three issues himself. He's meticulous like his father. And like his father, he's gotten into trouble because of what he wrote. She frets about the caning. How will it affect him? Richard never recovered from that fiasco with the now defunct *Singapore Morning Herald*. His report had caught her attention. In clear, crisp English, he had written about a university students' group, critical of the

Prime Minister and his cabinet. And he'd quoted her, and, based on something she had told him in confidence, he'd described her as one of the group's leaders. She stared at the report. There it was, her confidence purveyed and packed into a two-inch column of black print with a half-inch high headline. Below that was his byline: *I'm very sorry. Very very sorry. I had to break the news before* The Straits Times *does it.*

A single yellow rose and a box of Scottish nougat were proffered. She should have known better then. To think that her heart and forgiveness were so cheaply bought.

When the *Herald* was abruptly closed down by the government, he'd run like the rest of them to Malaysia, and then to Hong Kong before making his way back a year later after the fallout and debris had cleared, and he knew he wouldn't be detained again. Like a blind fool, she thought he had courage, and married him.

For god's sake! You're my wife! You can act for me. You're a teacher. You work only half a day. I don't have the time to meet these people.

You don't have the time or you don't have the guts?

He'd stormed out of their bedroom. He would rather pay fines, sometimes, heavy fines that they could barely afford, rather than deal with government authorities. She was the one who blundered through, argued, and fought with the Inland Revenue Authority, the Public Utilities Authority, the Housing Board Authority, the Property Tax Authority, the school authorities, the bank authorities, the hospital authorities – anyone and everyone in a position of authority. For years, she had refused to see it. Refused to see that he was cowering behind her. Perhaps *cowering* was too strong a word. But what else could she call it? Government officials unnerved him. But he wouldn't admit it. At home, he raved against the powers that be, the fools and tyrants who run this country. But put him in front of a government official, and he scraped and bowed.

Yes, yes, yes, I understand, sir. No problem, sir. Er ... er ... I'll ... I'll wait. So sorry. So sorry to bother you, mister, er, mister. Sir.

She suspected that it was his brush with Internal Security that had so unnerved him. But he refused to talk about it.

You were in there two weeks. What did they do to you? Please, Richard. You've got to talk it out.

Stop it, Joan.

He clammed up. She reckoned he was roughed up. She'd heard such stories whispered among friends. Sometimes, alone at night, she thought of him, imagining how they must've stripped him naked, made him sit on a block of ice or shone two hundred megawatt spotlights on him. Sleep deprived and stripped, he must have said or done things he was now ashamed of. For years, he'd suffered from insomnia and nightmares.

On the day of his release, his chief editor had told him to run. And so he ran. The next day, the chief editor himself was detained. The newspaper was closed down. Its publishing permit was withdrawn. Richard's parents told everyone they didn't know what their son had done, so they could not vouch for him, they said. His parents' reaction had shocked her. How could his parents wash their hands off their only son? But that was the madness of the sixties in Singapore when the air was choked with rumours of Black Ops CIA agents, and student activists as pawns of the Communist Front. Many fled the country in fear. Richard's father denounced them all, including his own son.

Why run if you've done nothing wrong? You say right or not?

But cowardice is in the Wong genes. It's in their bloody DNA. She fears her son will turn out to be like his father. Rave and rant in the safety of home. Cringe and shrink outside when authority appears. How could her son stay on in the school? He will not go against the school. He's refused to leave. Which mother wouldn't cry? She should stop it. She will call the school. Tell them she has changed her mind. She will rescind her agreement. She will withhold her consent. She will not let him become like his father.

'Mun! Where are you? Mun! Answer me! Open your door! Mun!'

*   *   *

1 October 2007. It's Mom's birthday. We're having dinner

in a little shophouse restaurant along Upper Bukit Timah Road. Just the two of us, the way she likes it. All mothers are suckers for this mother and son thing. She's fifty-five today. So I indulge her. Call her Momsy the way I used to as a kid and make her smile.

'I felt such a failure then.'

'Don't be so melodramatic, Mom. You didn't fail.'

'What do you mean melodramatic? It was traumatic.'

'For you, Mom. You were always so worried about face.'

'Now that's not a fair statement.'

'But it's true. You made a big fuss. See, you're still thinking about it after all these years. It wasn't such a big deal. I wasn't the only one caned.'

'It was a big deal for me, son. How could I have known it wasn't a big deal for you? We never spoke about it after that. You were so moody and morose as a teenager. Remember? You stopped talking to me after that.'

The waiter brings us our food. I've ordered a white wine for us as well.

'To your health, Mom.'

A pause. Then she starts again. 'Can I ask ...?'

'Must we do this? Is this your guilt or nostalgia? Oh, okay, okay.'

I give up. I relent. I haven't flown all the way back from New York to quarrel with her on her birthday. She lives alone. Poor Mom. She's bound to think of the past. Old people do. I know her. She will ponder and fret. She will recall my silence and the long hours I spent in my room as a teenager. She will say I didn't talk to her for days, for weeks, even months. She exaggerates sometimes. She tells me that I'd locked her out of my life; that her divorce took a toll on her poor boy, and many other such things. Mothers love to talk about their children's childhood. Tonight it's the caning in school. She never forgot the caning. Still, it's her birthday today so I will indulge her.

'So what do you want to know, Mom?'

'Why didn't you talk to me about it?'

'I don't know. It really wasn't a big deal. Anyway we weren't caned in the school hall.'

'You mean Harry Koh didn't carry out his threat?'

'No. I was given two strokes in class. Rajiv and Seng Huat had one stroke each.'

'That's not fair. How come you had two?'

'I was the editor. I was the one who decided what to publish.'

'So he gave you one more stroke.'

'Something like that,' I laugh. 'Mr Koh said he had to show that he supported the teacher. Said he had to protect his staff.'

'What? Protect his staff but not his students?'

'I didn't need his protection, Mom. I could protect myself. I protected my future, didn't I? I stayed. I didn't quit.'

'Because you were afraid to change school.'

'Good grief, Mom. Did you think so little of me then?'

'No. You know I didn't mean that. I was proud of you, son. I wanted you to change school because I couldn't stand that bully of a principal.'

'I wanted to handle it myself. I didn't want to have it on my record that I'd to quit school. Like I was expelled. Besides, I reckoned that bullies die. Eventually. Like all of us. Dad said, all tyrants have to die some day. All that the young have to do is to stay put and wait.'

'Did he say that?'

'He did. He even wrote about it in one of his articles. Write, he said. Write to keep the flame burning. It is Rajiv's mantra now. That guy's a bum but he's one of the best reporters in ST today.'

Mom is silent, thinking.

'Don't you see, Mom? Dad was right. Rajiv and I are still writing today. Huat's into Internet publishing. Where's Mr Koh?'

Mom almost falls off her chair, laughing. 'Who was it who said, "lose a battle, win a war?"' she giggles. 'Oh, this is absolutely my best birthday dinner ever.'

But I take that with a pinch of salt. Mom's humour has always been a bit off tangent. She taught literature before her retirement, and her favourite Shakespearean character was the Fool in *King Lear*.

'So you did go and see your dad. How come I didn't know?'

'I didn't tell you.'

'Oh.'

'Another thing I didn't tell you. Mr Koh coached me in maths for my "O" Level.'

'And you didn't you tell me that either?'

She wanted to know everything in those days. But she could only guess at what her son must have gone through during those difficult years. An only child torn between his parents. Was it her fault that he'd hidden from her his visits and consultations with his father and others? Was she too clingy? Too possessive? A divorced parent clinging to her child, afraid of losing him? I can see these thoughts racing through my mother's brain. To distract her I tell her about Dad.

'Dad said "happy birthday" to you. I spoke with him this morning.'

'How's he?'

'He's recovering from his op. He wants to continue his freelance writing. And he's learning to blog, he says.'

'Hmmm. Good for him. Did you tell him about Susannah?'

'Not yet. You're the first to know that your son's getting married.'

Mom's eyes light up at this. Although she will never admit it, she wants to come first in her son's life.

'I'm proud of you, son.'

'And I'm proud of you, Mom.'

Suchen Christine Lim's third novel, *Fistful of Colours*, was awarded the inaugural Singapore Literature Prize in 1993. Her fourth novel, *A Bit Of Earth* (2000) and a short-story collection, *The Man Who Wore His Wife's Sarong* (2007) were subsequently shortlisted for the same prize. A story from the above collection, *The Morning After*, was made into a film for Singapore television in 2008. Her other publications include two other novels, *Rice Bowl* and *Gift from the Gods*, a short play, a non-fiction book on Chinese immigrants, and several children's books. In 2010, she was featured in *Writing The City*, a series of short films commissioned by the British Council in Singapore.

She has been a judge for the Commonwealth Literature Prize (1999) and the Dymocks Singapore Literature Prize (2000). In 1997 she was awarded a Fulbright fellowship for the International Writers' Program at the University of Iowa, and in 2000, she was its International Writer-in-Residence. She also had writing residencies in the Philippines, Myanmar, South Korea, Australia and the UK. In 2011, she was Visiting Fellow in Creative Writing at the Nanyang Technological University (NTU), Singapore.

To learn more about Suchen Christine Lim, please visit: *www.suchenchristinelim.com*.

The Death

of a

Schoolmaster

Shashi Tharoor

I was ten years old when Achan came into his land. 'His' land – how easily one slips into the possessive pronoun. It was Amma's land, not even hers really, but her maternal uncle's. When he'd died heirless, our matrilineal system ensured that Amma inherited his estate. Which meant that Achan, as head of the family, suddenly became a landlord.

I still remember the little, three-roomed house we were living in when our fortunes so completely changed. There were six of us children then, banging our heads on the low doorway as we crowded into the kitchen for our breakfast *idlis*; only six, because my eldest sister had already been married off a year ago, and my youngest brother was not yet born. We would all sleep side by side on a large cotton mattress spread on the living-room floor (or rather, the floor of what I have since come to think of as the living-room, a word I had never heard in those days), with a thin sheet to protect us against the mosquitoes. The mosquitoes would buzz around our exposed faces, of course, so that we soon learned to tuck our heads too under the sheet. But all the pulling and the stretching involved in the six of us all keeping ourselves covered meant that often one person at the end got no sheet at all. That was usually my elder sister Thangam, who would curl up quietly on one side without complaint, just as she would forego her own meals in ensuring we all had enough to eat, or miss the bus for school in helping me to get ready for class. And when the sheet gave way one night to some rough tugging by my two elder brothers, leaving a rent down the middle, it was Thangam who slept under the hole, Thangam who saved her next few days' bus fare to buy the needle and thread we didn't have, Thangam who woke up early in the morning to sew the sheet before Achan saw it and beat us all. Those were days when simple sacrifices meant a great deal.

Achan was a schoolmaster then. He was a B.A., an educated man; he could read and write English. The cupboards in our house and in the small room he shared with Amma were crammed with books: advanced English readers, University textbooks, local editions (with impossibily small print) of well-known classics. They were dusty, termite-ridden, cracked and tearing, some without jackets, others carefully wrapped in newspaper covers, the paper yellowing and curling with age, but they were all read. My most enduring memory of Achan in those days is of him in the sagging easy-chair on the porch, peering in the light of a kerosene-lamp at the torn pages of an ageing book. That was before he had come to admit his need for spectacles, or to afford them. Amma would always say he was reading his eyes to ruin, but he would dismiss her with a snort, or ask her to get him a cup of tea instead of bothering him.

Amma was very much the downtrodden wife in those days. When I think of her at that time, I am still startled by the difference between her then and the bustling, vigorous matriarch of later years. Some women grow only in widowhood. As a wife, Amma was quite content to live in Achan's shadow. He had married her, a barely educated orphan with only a prosperous uncle to her name, when she was fifteen. She had known no other brother, or father, or male friend, or instructor, and it as obvious that for her Achan combined all these roles. This didn't mean that she was devoid of individual spirit or conviction, for the children were frequently at the receiving end of her whiplash tongue. It was just that whenever Achan was around, her habitual manner was one of compliant diffidence.

There were so many gaps between them. Age: he was thirty when he married her, double her age, and even as time passed, the fifteen years loomed forbiddingly between them like the shadow of an unscalable cliff. Sex: he was a man in a man's world, equipped to cope with its mysteries; she had gone from the insignificance and fears of a fatherless girlhood into the insignificance and security of an arranged marriage. Education: she had eight grades of schooling, enough to give her a fine, precise, rounded handwriting in the only language she knew, Malayalam; he was the only graduate in the family, a man of learning, steeped in books. The wisdom of age, the assurance of manhood, the knowledge of scholarship, all were his. To these qualities she could only juxtapose her innocence, her uncertainties, her ignorance.

But they were happy together. Happiness can only come when poverty is not equated to want. My father earned only (how easy it is to say 'only' now) seventy-five rupees a month for his labours, but he never felt he should want more. Others in the village, many without his B.A., would crowd onto trains and travel long distances to seek clerical jobs in cities like Bombay, which paid them twice as much. They would subsist in hovels and send the bulk of their earnings home to their families in Kerala. A neighbour once wondered aloud whether Achan too could not do better by taking the typing course offered in the next town, and going to work as a stenographer in Bombay like so many husbands and sons of her acquaintances. The vehemence of his reaction rapidly established for her and anyone else who might have been listening (as I was) that neither the skill nor the profession concerned was worthy of a gentleman's consideration. In any case, it never crossed Amma's mind to urge any change upon Achan. He was what he was and it was her duty to serve him and raise his family. That was enough for her.

When the inheritance came they were caught off guard. I suppose they must have known, in some recess of their minds, that Valiamaman's assets would one day be theirs, especially as the years went on and he failed to acquire or produce other heirs. But Amma was not the kind of person to think very much about it and Achan had no place for such prospects in his world of books and school papers. I imagine that, in any case, they were not expecting anything quite so soon. Valiamaman was an active sixty at the time of his sudden death, in circumstances which were never satisfactorily explained to us children. Later inquiry and surmise have led me to conclude he had a seizure when closeted with the buxom young maidservant whom Amma dismissed soon after we moved in. He was an energetic man to the end.

The move was traumatic. It meant a major displacement from our little town, where Achan taught at the government high school, to our ancestral village over fifteen miles away. It meant changing the habits of a lifetime, bus schedules, games, friends. It meant coping with the mysteries of a thirty-five-room house where suddenly each of us had our own bedroom-cum-study. We could never come to terms with this unwanted gift of privacy and would end up, as before, sleeping side by side on our cotton mattress in the grand front room where Valiamaman used to receive the visits of his fellow *zamindars* in more prosperous times.

And for Achan it meant the unfamiliar responsibility of sixty acres of paddy fields, scattered over two villages forty miles apart. His land.

He had to give up the school. For one thing he was no longer down the road from it. He would have had to walk nearly an hour, catch an unreliable bus and walk ten minutes again, none of which would have been good for either his dignity or his feet. For another, he had to keep an eye on his land, attend to details of its ploughing, sowing, irrigation and harvesting, employ contract labour, pay the government levies, apply for fertilizer, arrange for the sale of the produce. It was a full-time job.

It was also too much for him. I don't know when I began to realize it, but it became apparent before long that Achan couldn't cope. He would return from a hot, dusty day in the fields, exhausted and irritable. He would delve suspiciously into the dinner Amma laid out for him, and complain uncharacteristically about the vegetables in the *avial* or the sourness of the *thayiru*, bark at a few of us, and attempt to seek solace in his easy-chair. But no sooner had he turned a page of whatever book he had picked up than someone would emerge on the veranda, hands folded in supplication, to raise some problem about the land. And Achan would put his book down in despair and try to arrive at a decision on some matter he knew less about than his visitor.

It was obvious, too, that Achan's lack of aptitude for farming was taking its toll on the family finances. We children were never encouraged to think about money, an inhibition which in the past hadn't prevented us from realizing we hadn't any. But Amma let us know early on that if we had come up in the world to possess the largest house in the village, with our own mango tree and vegetable garden, we didn't have much other than some tumble-down furniture to go with it. We grew more or less whatever we needed to eat, but money for everything from clothes to bus-fare had to come from the sales of our paddy, and Amma made it clear there wasn't very much of that after salaries and levies had been paid and the upkeep of the house attended to. Under Achan's management the returns from the farm seemed to decline. The tell-tale signs appeared in the weeks when the profits from the previous harvest had dwindled and the expenses for the new sowing began to mount. At these times, our milk would turn watery, the clothes would be given less often to the washerwoman, a special occasion would no longer be celebrated by a bullock cart trip to the cinema-theatre in the nearest town.

It was during one of these periods that Thangam fell ill.

Thangam, who helped Amma do without a full-time servant by working in the kitchen before and after school; Thangam, who attended to everything from my scraped knee to the weekly puja offerings; Thangam, who silently bore the brunt of Achan's irrational anger for anything that had gone wrong in the house; Thangam fell ill, and it was as if our world had collapsed around us. She stumbled one day in the kitchen, dropping a precious pan of boiling milk in her fall to the floor, and it was more the split milk than the fall that convinced me something was seriously wrong. Amma ran in alarm and anger to her, but after one look at Thangam's face she brought the hand she had raised for a slap gently down upon her daughter's forehead. I was in the kitchen by then, and I could see the alarm on her face.

'You're very hot, my child,' she said quietly. 'You have a fever.'

'Nonsense, mother, it's just the heat of the kitchen,' Thangam retorted, but in a voice so weak I knew she was lying.

'Go and lie down, my dear,' Amma said. 'I can manage in here.' And despite Thangam's protests she was bundled off, with me in tow.

When Achan came home that night he was initially too wrapped up in his problems to notice that anything was amiss. Then it struck him that it was I who was helping my mother serve his dinner. 'Where's Thangam?' he asked. 'Has she already gone to sleep?'

'No, she is not well, poor child,' Amma replied. 'She had a fever and I've asked her to lie down.'

'What have you given her? Has she eaten anything?'

'No, she didn't want any food.'

'Medicine? Did you give her something for the fever?'

'I didn't know where you kept the medicine. I thought I would wait for you to come.'

Father washed his hands and went to Thangam. She was shivering uncontrollably under the thin sheet. Drops of perspiration stood on her brow like beads fallen off a broken chain.

'You should have called a doctor,' he said accusingly to Amma.

'How could I? I don't even know where to find one or what his name is. I waited for you to come,' she repeated despairingly.

'It's too late for tonight. Tomorrow, the boy must go to Dr Parameshwar in Nemmara.' He gave me instructions on how to get to the doctor's clinic in the nearby town. 'Ask the doctor to come here.'

'But how can we possibly afford to pay ...?' my mother began.

'I'll find a way,' Achan said grimly. 'Get the doctor. I have to go early tomorrow to our fields in Shoranur. I may not be back till very late. If the work keeps me too long and I cannot get a bus it could even be tomorrow afternoon before I return. But don't worry. I am sure the doctor will take good care of Thangam.'

I slept next to my sister that night. Her skin was so hot I recoiled from her in shock. She dozed fitfully, her body racked by shudders. Occasionally she cried deliriously in words I could not understand.

In the morning I ran through the paddy fields to the nearest bus-stop. It took me twenty minutes a normal morning; today I did it in ten. There I waited in an agony of frustration for the bus to Nemmara. When it came it was full, but I clambered onto the tail-board and clung on in desperation throughout the bumpy ride. My father's directions were good; I found the clinic without great difficulty. There were a number of patients in the queue and in the waiting room. I tried to barge in to see the doctor but was sharply reprimanded by a nurse. Each moment seemed to drag by until finally I was ushered into the doctor's chamber.

'My - sister's - very - sick - you - must - come - and - see - her,' I burst out in one breath.

The doctor laughed. He was a kindly man, with a round face and a bushy, black moustache. 'Now, now, hold on there a minute, son,' he said. 'What exactly is the matter with your sister?'

I told him. His face became grave. 'Yes, I think I must see her,' he agreed. 'Can you bring her here?'

'But it's impossible!' I expostulated. 'She can hardly sit up. And we – could not bring her in our bullock cart.' I did not add that we could not afford a taxi from the town.

He reflected for a moment. 'All right, I shall come,' he said finally. I can still remember the sense of triumph and relief which his words produced in me. 'But not just yet. I have all these patients to see.' He gestured towards the queue outside.

'But you must come now,' I pleaded stubbornly. 'My sister cannot wait.'

'She will have to,' he said firmly. 'These people have all been waiting.'

'But this is different! She may – she may – die,' I whispered the last word, confronting its horror for the first time.

He looked at me in exasperation.

'I shall not leave this room till you agree to come with me,' I said very quietly.

He came, his anger dissolving in tolerant laughter. And Thangam didn't die. When we got home, I saw to my surprise a familiar figure sitting by Thangam's bedside, stroking her hair. My father.

He didn't say a word in response to my look of astonishment. But after the doctor had examined Thangam, administered his medication, told us all would be well in a few days and left us with his prescription, my father explained what he had decided to Amma.

'I came back,' he said simply, tousling my hair and sounding defensive. 'And I'm not going to go again. It is madness, travelling all the way to Shoranur every other day. And it is not as if my going there makes a lot of difference either. My place is here, with you and my children. Balan Nair, your Valiamaman's old retainer, has offered to manage these fields for us. He will give us a specific portion of the harvest, and attend to all the daily chores. It will save us a lot of trouble.'

'But – how can you give it all to him?' Amma was incredulous. 'More than half our land is there, in the Shoranur fields.'

'I'm not *giving* anything to him, woman,' Achan rejoined irritably. 'The land is still ours. He is just going to run it for us, that's all. And I can keep an eye on the smaller fields around our village. Nathan is old enough to help me.' Nathan was my oldest brother. It was obvious he was not going to amount to very much at school. My father had clearly made a wise decision.

Things got a lot better after that. Balan Nair took

complete charge of running the fields, and though later his duties were paid at intermittent intervals and he increasingly seemed to have new reasons for not giving Achan all that we expected, we still had an assured income without Achan having to lift a finger for it. I still remember Balan Nair's frequent visits to Achan, a clean white cloth flung over one shoulder, his head bending so low in respect over his folded hands it looked as if he was going to drink from them. Achan was happy and relaxed. He had more time for his books now as Nathan gradually took over control of the closer fields. My brother had that capacity to alternate between seasons of hectic activity and periods of enforced idleness that in our country characterizes the rustic life. Achan was able to leave virtually everything to him – and, of course, to Balan Nair.

This left Achan a lot more time for me. He would let me into his 'book-room', as we children called it, and turn a casual browse into a magic world of instruction and enlightenment. He taught me, without the drudgery of a classroom, things I would never have been able to learn in school. He introduced me to the English language, to the pleasures of literature and the perils of philosophy. When he caught me straying into a card-game with my brother's farmer friends, he would pull me out on some pretext and shame me with his disapproval. As to the new vocation the inheritance had given us, Achan never let me have anything to do with it. The first time I attempted to accompany Nathan *etta* to the field, he stopped me. 'That's not the world I want you to inhabit,' he told me fiercely.

'Leave the fields to your brother, you understand? And never let me catch you going there again.' His interdiction was so total I was the only male in my family who didn't know the way to our *kalam* from the house.

The years passed in tranquillity. Thangam, restored, already an able housewife in her teens, was married to the son of a landed family. Achan did not have to borrow for the dowry, as he had had to do for my eldest sister. Another child was born, my youngest brother, the only birth in the big house. The event seemed to signify a rebirth for Amma too. She began to acquire more authority in her role, as Achan slipped more and more into complaisance. I did very well at school and was admitted to the government Victoria College in Palghat, the district capital thirty miles away. It was clear I was the one destined to follow Achan's educated footsteps.

Those were the turbulent years in Kerala. All the big issues of the day seemed to be emerging in the microcosm of our little state – communism versus bourgeois democracy, parliamentary politics versus revolution, capitalism versus socialism, free education versus scholarly privilege, agrarianism versus industrialization. Tempers heated rapidly on our campuses: conflicts erupted over words and were fought over bodies. I was caught up irresistibly in the mood of the times. I had the talents of a 'leader': a loud voice, a way with words and a willingness to employ both in the service of my interests. I joined an opposition party and rose rapidly in it. Before long, while I was still in my mid-twenties, I was awarded the party's ticket to contest the elections to the state assembly.

I went home in a mood of jubilation to prepare my campaign. It was there that the first news of misfortune reached me. Achan had developed some sort of mysterious pain that left him virtually crippled. The local doctors seemed to be able to do nothing to relieve his discomfort, and could only attribute it to a particularly severe form of rheumatism.

I wanted to help, but I was too much in the fray of my political battle. I left it to my brothers to investigate the matter further, and embarked upon my electioneering.

I had early arrived at a populist brand of politics, which suited my rhetorical style and my ideological convictions. My familiarity with the ideas of equality and freedom had first come from the crumbling pages of Tom Paine, Mill and Rousseau on my father's bookshelves. But I had been able to update their ideas by the inevitable university acquaintance with Marx and a diligent reading of Nehru. Today I spoke eloquently against priests and businessmen, and for free schooling and land reform. The latter was an issue that rapidly caught the imagination of my predominantly rural constituency. 'Land to the people!' I declaimed. 'The tillers must benefit from their toil! Down with the landlord exploiters!'

My popularity was rapidly achieved. There was I, the educated, city-college product of a good family, speaking up for the people's rights. My father had instilled in me the view that ideas were unrelated to life: they inhabited a rarefied world of books, not of men. 'You are what you believe, my son,' he would often say. Since philosophy was a diagnosis, not a prescription, for life, beliefs did not have to be reconciled to behaviour. The country's most prominent communists were themselves prosperous elitists. I thus saw no contradiction between my convictions and my context; I thought I was merely going one step further by translating my views into votes. And I did it well. With my oratorical skills I was able to give expression to the inarticulate grievances of the landless peasant. His work would be rewarded, I promised. Land would go to the tiller. There would be a ceiling on how much property one person could own.

I received the news of my victory at the polls the same evening as the laboratory reports came in on my father. Achan had cancer. His pains would never disappear.

I can remember the shock. I can recall the euphoria. I am no longer sure whether one succeeded in crowding out the other.

Achan was dying while I was to attend my first session of the state legislature. 'Go, my son,' he said to me when I turned to him in anguished farewell. 'I am proud of you. You and what you stand for represent the future. Do not hold it up for the past.'

Achan was flown to Bombay, where my eldest sister and her husband lived, for specialist treatment in a cancer hospital. I promised to go there as soon as I could complete my first major task at the assembly. It was the Land Reform Bill. I was one of its prime movers.

When I got to Bombay the news was all bad. Achan's cancer had made alarming progress. Only prolonged and expensive treatment, using equipment and medicine that would have to be flown in from abroad, could forestall the inevitable. There seemed to be no way we could afford that.

'But we can,' said Amma excitedly. 'We *can* afford it. All we have to do is sell the land we've let out to Balan Nair. We don't need it any more. Almost all the children are settled – we can live off the fields in our own village. Why, we can probably sell the land to Balan Nair himself.'

I agreed, and volunteered to rush back to Kerala to arrange the transaction.

Balan Nair received me in his house. As I stepped across the smooth, new, cement pathway into the freshly painted coolness of his living-room, I realized with a shock why his payments to Achan had been so irregular. He had clearly done very well out of the arrangement.

'New house?' I couldn't resist asking as he ushered me to a chair.

'Built it last year,' he admitted proudly. 'We have had a few good harvests.' He sat, too, on a slightly higer chair, and then it struck me: with my father he had always stood.

'It is about those harvests that I have come to speak to you,' I said awkwardly, accepting a servant's proffered cup of tea. 'As you may know, my father is not very well.'

'I have heard,' he replied. 'Very sad news.' He didn't sound sad at all.

'Achan requires some specialized treatment in Bombay, which is going to cost a lot of money,' I began. I paused, not knowing exactly how to phrase it.

'Have you come to me for money?' he asked abruptly.

'Of course not.' I could feel the colour rising to my cheeks. 'I have come to tell you that we wish to sell our land here in Shoranur. That is the only way we can raise the funds we need to pay the hospital.'

'Very interesting.' Balan Nair said, flicking absently at a passing fly with the loose end of his shoulder-cloth.

'I thought you might be interested, perhaps, in purchasing it.' I cast a look around the evident prosperity of his surroundings. 'I am sure you can afford it, and we will of course arrange a fair price.'

'I would be very interested indeed,' Balan Nair replied, 'if you had any land to offer me in Shoranur. But I didn't know you owned any land here.'

At first I thought he hadn't understood. 'You know the land I mean,' I said a trifle impatiently. 'The land my father let you use, here.'

'I know no such thing,' Balan Nair responded equably. And then it hit me. He was going to deny the arrangement ever existed.

'You mean ...' I spluttered, rage battling incomprehension. The words wouldn't come; they tripped over barriers of confused thought and fell soundlessly in my mind.

'I mean that the land I use here is mine,' he said. 'I have tilled it for the last fifteen years. Last week I registered my possession of it, quite legally, under the new Land Reform Act. I believe you know something about the Act?'

The question rendered me speechless. I had never associated the Act with him. Land reform, in my mind, had nothing to do with the likes of Balan Nair. It was an idea redolent with images of half-naked labourers, the sweat glistening on their black muscular bodies, their voices raised in a raucous clamour for justice. Balan Nair didn't fit the concept, or the cause.

'Land to the tiller. Tenancy rights. A well-drafted piece of legislation, that. You must read it sometime.' The white teeth, the white shoulder-cloth, mocked me in their triumphant brightness. 'It provides for a ceiling of twenty acres per person, provided the land is actually used by the owner. I have registered twenty acres in my name, eighteen in my wife's. We propose to continue to cultivate this land. *Our* land.'

He gestured to the maidservant to fill up my cup. I thought of his hired labourers outside, bending in the sun over the ruts in the fields. Land to the tiller: the slogan had found its reality.

'I believe you know, better than most people, that it would be futile to make an issue of this,' he added. 'You wouldn't stand a chance in any court of law.' He smiled indulgently at me. 'And now, is there any *other* land you would like to sell …?'

Though I knew it was hopeless, I tried to have something done. I called up lawyers, spoke to officials, even tried to press some of my political connections into service. In the end I realized what I should have known all along: nothing could be done. Change had come, and it was immutable. The law, and justice, were on Balan Nair's side.

Achan came home from Bombay. I had offered to take a loan which I would pay back later, but he had refused to hear of it. I tried to persuade Amma to take it, but she was too proud. If their land could not pay for Achan's treatment, they would do without it. I accompanied them back home in a torment of guilt and self-reproach.

Achan died slowly, his pain eased by stronger and stronger tranquillizers. In one of his last few lucid moments, he whispered hoarsely into my ear as I leaned my head towards his gaunt and shrunken face. 'Have no regrets, my son,' he said. 'I don't have any. My time has come. The foreign treatment would only have prolonged my pain. Do not blame yourself about anything. What you did was what you believed in. Do that always, and you will always be right.'

He died later with a book in his hands, trying though the blurred mists of his suffering to read some well-worn truth, reinforce another belief. I was there to slip the volume from his hands and gently close his tired eyes. I knew that, thanks to him, mine would always be open.

An elected Member of Parliament, former Minister of State for External Affairs and former Under-Secretary-General of the United Nations, Shashi Tharoor is the prize-winning author of twelve books, both fiction and non-fiction, including the classic *The Great Indian Novel* (1989), *India: From Midnight to the Millennium* (1997), *Nehru: The Invention of India* (2003) and *The Elephant, the Tiger and the Cellphone: Reflections on India in the 21st Century* (2007).

A widely-published critic, commentator and columnist (including for *The Hindu*, *The Times of India* and *Newsweek*), Shashi Tharoor served the United Nations during a 29-year career in refugee work, peacekeeping, the Secretary-General's office and heading communications and public information. In 2006 he was India's candidate to succeed Kofi Annan as UN Secretary-General, and emerged a strong second out of seven contenders. He has won India's highest honour for Overseas Indians, the Pravasi Bharatiya Samman, and numerous literary awards, including a Commonwealth Writers' Prize.

For more on Shashi Tharoor, please see: *www.tharoor.in*.

Because I Tell

Felix Cheong

Where I hide, I see stars. So many, many twinkle, twinkle little stars. How I wonder what they are. Mama says they are God's eyes. I say that's why God sees everything. Mama laughs loud and kisses my head. I remember because she doesn't kiss me for a long time.

I count the stars. I finish counting at 15 yesterday. Now I start at 16. I think, they are my birthday candles. I am 16 years old today! Happy birthday to Ben, happy birthday to me! I make a wish. Then I close my eyes slowly, blowing one candle, one candle, one candle. I must keep secret my wish. If I tell, I will not get my wish. That's why Cheche says Dada won't come home. Because I tell.

Where I hide, I am cold. I have many, many leaves like a blanket up to my face. I sleep on brown grass. The dry leaves tickle my backside like I remember how Uncle Timmy tickles me one time. He holds me on the bed and I pee in my dark blue shorts. He laughs loud and says he also wants to pee. But he doesn't go to the toilet. He says, 'This is a secret.'

My yellow Brazil T-shirt is dirty. Dada gives it one time to me. He likes football very much. When he finishes work, he takes me to the green grass downstairs to play football. I kick the ball to him and he kicks it back to me. He says this is father-and-son talk. Sometimes he kicks the ball very far and I run to find it.

Dada takes me one time to the National Stadium to watch a football game. So many, many people shout. They shout 'Referee *kayu*!' They shout 'Goal!' I think, football is a fun game because people can shout. When I play with Cheche at home and we shout, Mama scolds. She says, 'You want to wake up the dead?' I hear many, many people shout now in the National Stadium and they must wake up the dead. Where are the dead? I also shout 'Goal!' but people look at me. Dada laughs loud and says not yet. It is only an offside. I shout 'Goal!' only when Dada shouts 'Goal!'

When the football game finishes, the man next to Dada shakes his hand. I see he gives Dada money. I am scared of this man. He is short with yellow hair and he has painting of dragons on his right arm. The dragons grow bigger when he moves his arm. He smokes many, many times and comes to my house many times. He says to Dada, 'Next week, more.' Dada tells me to keep secret. Then we take bus number 16 to Lucky Plaza and he buys me a yellow Brazil T-shirt. He also has a Brazil T-shirt. I wear number 11 and he wears number 10. He says Brazil is his favourite team because he makes money one time when they win the World Cup. I ask if many people drink from the World Cup. He laughs loud and says, 'Only God can drink from the World Cup.' I think, God cannot be very thirsty.

When we go home, Mama asks Dada where he gets money to buy Ben a Brazil T-shirt. I say the dragon man gives Dada money. Then Mama shouts at Dada and he shouts back. They shout for a long time. They throw things on the floor. Mama throws her favourite cup. Dada throws my favourite cup. I am scared and I cry. Now I cannot drink from my favourite cup.

Cheche takes me to the bedroom and closes the door. She says, 'Why do you have to tell Mama? See what you did?' I say I forget it is a secret. Cheche says, 'You always forget. You were born stupid. You will always be stupid.'

I say I am not stupid. I keep secrets. I never tell Mama Cheche takes Terence one time to her bedroom. I never tell Mama Terence kisses Cheche and holds her on the bed. I never tell Mama Terence tickles Cheche and they wear no clothes and they laugh loud. Cheche hits my face. She goes out of the house but forgets to take her keys. I cry and I put a pillow on my pain. Too many, many secrets to forget!

When I wake up, I want to say sorry to Dada. I want to tell him I am born stupid and I will always be stupid. Many, many days, I wait at the green grass downstairs with the football. I kick it very far and I run to find it. I wait at home. I ask Cheche where is Dada. She doesn't talk to me. I ask Mama where is Dada. She says he is dead. I cry I want Dada but Mama scolds. She says, 'I take care of you and you only want that useless man? You are ungrateful!' When Mama goes to work, I shout 'Dada!' many, many times at home to wake up the dead. I want to have father-and-son talk. But I don't see him.

My Brazil T-shirt is very dirty now. My dark blue shorts are also dirty. I see ants everywhere on my legs. I am scared Mama scolds when I get home. She says, 'You think I don't have anything to do? Can't you keep yourself clean? I have to hand-wash your clothes everyday. Look at my hands. They are bleeding!'

I don't want Mama's hands to bleed. I am scared she dies like Jesus. His hands bleed all the time in church. I am scared to look at him. I ask Mama one time if Jesus hand-washes many, many clothes. She scolds and says I talk rubbish. She wants me to kneel in front of Jesus and say sorry. I kneel down and say Jesus, sorry I talk rubbish. I don't know why I am born stupid. I don't know why I tell secrets. Jesus looks at me and bleeds.

I keep myself clean because I don't want Mama to hand-wash many, many clothes and bleed like Jesus. I wash myself three times everyday. After I wake up, I wash my face. After I go to the toilet, I wash my hands. After I have my dinner, I wash my body.

But now, I smell bad like the drains in Geylang. We go there one time to eat claypot rice. Me, Mama, Cheche and Uncle Timmy. I remember the bad smell, like old eggs from our old fridge. One time, I break three old eggs to let the chickens come out. Cheche says the baby chickens are locked up because they are naughty. Like how Mama locks up me one time because I am naughty. She says, 'You have to open them to rescue them.' When I open the three eggs, I see no baby chickens. Only uncooked omelette. Mama scolds when she comes home. She says I waste food. Then she scolds Cheche but she laughs loud.

I ask Mama why the drains in Geylang smell bad like old eggs from our old fridge. She says it's because Geylang hides many people's dirty secrets. Many people go to Geylang to do things they can't do in the day. That's why it smells bad. After that, I stop eating old eggs. I don't want to smell bad like I hide secrets. If I smell bad and I wash myself four times everyday, Mama scolds. She says, 'You waste water like that, Bedok Reservoir will run dry tomorrow morning.'

I don't want Bedok Reservoir to run dry. I like it there. I go there with Uncle Timmy sometimes. He comes to our house many, many times after Dada never comes home. He is a tall and big man like Dada. He smokes many, many times like the dragon man. He doesn't go to work like Dada. He doesn't have father-and-son talk with me at the green grass downstairs. He doesn't take me to the National Stadium. Uncle Timmy sleeps in Mama's bedroom now.

I go to the toilet one time at night in Mama's bedroom. I see Uncle Timmy holds Mama on the bed and tickles her. They wear no clothes and they laugh loud. I pull down my dark blue shorts and I say I want to pee. Mama shouts, 'Why didn't you knock? Why can't you use the toilet in the kitchen?' I say I am scared. 'Scared of what? The dead? I can't even have privacy in my own house. I don't know what I did to give birth to a stupid boy like you. You will always be stupid. You will always be useless like your good-for-nothing father. Now get out of the house!'

Uncle Timmy doesn't say anything. Cheche is not at home. I want to pee but I go out of the house. I am scared, I cry but I walk and walk to Bedok Reservoir.

Where I hide, I hear Bedok Reservoir. I lie down and count the stars. I think, if God sees everything, he must see everybody's secrets. He must keep secret many, many secrets. He must smell like old eggs from our old fridge.

I am 16 today and make a wish now. But I will not tell.

Felix Cheong, named by Readers' Digest as the 29th Most Trusted Singaporean of 2010, is the author of seven books, including four collections of poetry, two teen detective novels and a non-fiction anthology of interviews. He has also written two plays and edited a volume of essays. His latest anthology of verse is *Sudden in Youth: New and Selected Poems*.

Felix has been invited to read at writers' festivals all over the world: Edinburgh, West Cork, Austin, Sydney, Brisbane, Christchurch, Hong Kong, Chengdu, Kuala Lumpur, Ubud, Bangalore and Singapore. In 2004, he was nominated for the Singapore Literature Prize, and in 2000, he received the National Arts Council's Young Artist of the Year for Literature Award.

Felix completed his Master of Philosophy in Creative Writing at the University of Queensland in 2002 and is currently an adjunct lecturer.

A Life Elsewhere

Jaishree Misra

It would be no exaggeration to say that Manichettan was the most beloved of us all. Not merely amongst us cousins but also to Ammumma, our maternal grandmother, who never even attempted to hide the fact that she adored Manichettan just that tiny bit more than she did the rest of her multiplying brood.

Nobody minded particularly. For one, Manichettan was the oldest in our generation and 'leader of the pack' as our maternal uncle sometimes said. Even my brother once explained in a sage-like manner why he thought all the grown-ups liked Manichettan the most: 'Manichettan was already *there*, you see, before we all came along,' as though that was explanation enough. In my view, the reason for which Manichettan did not invite jealousy from the rest of us was because he was so willing to use his good offices with the elders to keep the more troublesome of us out of trouble. That, going by my experiences at school, was a rare quality in any human being.

Like the time I was about six and had fallen out of the *jambakkya* tree while trying to get to the sour pink fruit that was forbidden just before lunch. Hearing my howls and Amma's subsequent shouts, Manichettan came running up. 'I made her do it, Kunyamma,' he said, his forehead wrinkling with the effort of lying, 'It was a challenge, you see, to be the first to gather the biggest *jambakkya* for me.' Which was not true at all: Manichettan didn't even like *jambakkya*, preferring the sweet juiciness of the papayas and pineapples that grew on the southern side of the garden. It looked like Amma didn't believe him either, going by the way she quirked her eyebrow at this unlikely story; but the very fact that Manichettan had sprung so stoutly to my defence seemed to make the annoyance seep instantly out of her. She stood watching, trying unsuccessfully to purse her lips and maintain the sour look on her face as Manichettan picked me up off the gravel and used the edge of my chemise to wipe the tears and sweat off my face.

I remembered that incident many years later, two years ago precisely in fact, when I was studying for my MBA. Our lecturer was saying something about the culture of workplaces being set by attitudes that trickled down from senior management and, oddly, it was Manichettan I suddenly thought of. In a curious fashion, Manichettan, being the oldest cousin, seemed sort of directly responsible for the bonhomie that so firmly knitted us all together. Although Ammumma's *tharavaadu* was not a workplace, it certainly had the hot-house atmosphere of one when everyone gathered during the summer holidays, five crowded weeks that could quite easily have descended into quarrels and factions had the dynamics been different. In a household where a dozen mattresses were lined up in the dining hall every night for the children to sleep, queues formed for bathrooms at crucial hours and womenfolk spent inordinate amounts of time getting vast quantities of food prepared in the kitchen, it was only natural that irritations should pop up. In all honesty, it was the grown-ups who seemed to indulge in the occasional bickering, the usual flashpoints being when the men got into animated political discussions in the front verandah or when Ammumma was seen to favour one daughter over another. But we kids were almost without exception a united bunch – all thirteen of us which, in hindsight, seems a most remarkable feat. Of course we got into the odd scrap or two; but it was always short-lived and Manichettan was always peace-maker, especially on those long hot afternoons when the grown-ups who presided over our world sank into the sleep of the dead, confident of Manichettan's abilities to keep us all in check. 'He will be a high-ranking United Nations official someday, wait and see,' Acha often said, ruffling Manichettan's shock of springy black hair.

Well, it wasn't to the United Nations that Manichettan went. Instead, he moved to Singapore, having been offered a job with a sea freight company after he had finished his engineering degree in Trivandrum. It was around the same time that our massive summertime gatherings came to an end too. Ammumma died in 1995 and Apoopa followed her a mere three months after, seeming unable to cope without

91

his efficient wife by his side. More than that, it was the sale of their old house that quite simply left us without a place to gather. The next generation's houses were scattered all around the country and were, in any case, far too small to accommodate more than one extra family or two. My grandparents had left the *tharavaadu* jointly to my mother and her four sisters while Gopumama got given the rice fields. After many convoluted discussions, it became clear that it would be most expeditious and convenient all round if the old house was sold and the money distributed. Everyone had diverse financial needs and no one particularly wanted to be stuck with such a crumbling old edifice. It fetched a good price from a Dubai party whose plan was to raze the house to make room for a shopping complex, and that brought our holidays in the old homestead to a final close.

I missed those days terribly, although I was aware that, by then, there was an element of 'moving on' anyway, some of my older cousins being college students by this time and too busy to spend the long holidays playing childish games. But I longed for so many things: my grandmother's brisk presence, her rambling tree-filled garden and the dark cool of a cavernous kitchen that endlessly churned out vast quantities of food and was always ringing with female laughter. Even now, all it takes is the whiff of *pazham-pori* being fried to bring it all rushing back and, suddenly, I am seated again at Ammumma's pitted wooden table, offering to swap my crispy bit with the oozing caramelized banana centre that I preferred. With Manichettan, I didn't have to negotiate swaps though as he was always swift to offer me half the banana part of his *pazham-pori* anyway. He was that selfless, and so it should be no surprise that I later did for him what I did.

As the months passed, we found that the end of our family holidays were not as big a loss as they could have been, given that the Internet Age had arrived concurrently. Suddenly we were able to stay in touch via a Cousins-Net created by Sumichechi, the techie amongst us. She was also the first to discover Facebook some years later and promptly created a Cousins-Account on that too. Someone posted a picture that was taken back in the old *tharavaadu* when I was about seven; an old black and white snap of thirteen grubby children lined up and squinting into the camera, the younger ones wearing what was then our standard uniform of cotton home-made chemises grimy with mud and sweat. Other pictures followed, now all in colour: more recent group photos taken at weddings and engagement ceremonies and others of proliferating nuclear families and new babies and graduation ceremonies in far corners of the world.

Manichettan in Singapore wasn't actually on Facebook (stating something high-minded that I didn't quite understand about the principles of privacy), but he was a diligent emailer and, whenever he sent anyone a special message or a photograph, he didn't seem to mind that the recipient would instantly upload it on our Facebook Page so that the rest could also see how our oldest cousin was getting on.

From those pictures, I saw that Manichettan still had his thin, wiry frame, quite unlike that of his brother and mine, especially seeing how both Vinoochettan and Baluchettan had ballooned, post-marriage.

I had been out of touch with Manichettan for a long time which was clearly my fault as I knew that all it would take was one email for him to send me a long and solicitous reply. I had been busy with my MBA and then with the job I had landed soon after with a major cosmetics company. So information on family events now came delivered mostly via Amma who took great pains to keep me updated with news of weddings and other achievements during our Sunday evening telephone conversations. There wasn't much about Manichettan except that he was doing very well in his job and had promised his mother that he would be ready to commit to marriage by the time he turned thirty. But his thirtieth birthday had come and gone and there was still no sign of a wedding.

'Perhaps he wants to marry a pretty little Singaporean but is too scared of Valliamma to break the news,' I laughed, only half-joking.

My attempt at humour got short shrift from Amma: 'Don't make fun like that. We are not such an old-fashioned family. Didn't we all accept Vinoo's Simran, just like that, with no problem? Poor Valliamma and Valliachen even went all the way to Ludhiana to take part in the Punjabi wedding. It was so cold there that Valliamma said she had to wear a cap and two-two sweaters at night, even under the woollen blankets.'

'Of course everyone accepted Simran,' I retorted, 'but that's because Vinoochettan has always done exactly as he pleases, Amma. And no one was even half expecting him to marry a girl the family chose anyway. He's not like Manichettan at all. In fact, for brothers, it's amazing how different the two of them are. If Manichettan felt his parents would be unhappy with any of his decisions, he would die a thousand deaths before letting it happen.'

Amma must have recognized the truth in my words for she said nothing in reply.

I understood of course why Manichettan's on-going single status would be cause for concern amongst my mother's siblings, and it became a much-discussed subject. '*Paavam* Mani,' they said, perhaps rightly, 'No wife to cook for him in Singapore. Is it any wonder he is so thin?'

'No one cooks in Singapore, Valliamma,' I tried to reassure my aunt once. 'In fact, Manichettan said in one of his emails that the street food is so fresh and so cheap that most Singaporeans don't bother running kitchens at all.'

It was not a clever thing to say. 'Street food!' Valliamma yelped as though in pain. Then she sounded tearful, 'Imagine my Mani being reduced to eating street food. How he loves my *aviyal* and *theeyal*. And just think – there is no one to even make him a cup of tea over there in Singapore.'

My mother rushed in to patch over my thoughtlessness. 'Yes he definitely needs a wife, and we are all here to help him find the best one.' The siblings nodded in agreement. It wasn't all about food and hot cups of tea; there were other important considerations too which couldn't be voiced before youngsters, their expressions seemed to say. This conversation was taking place the night before my own brother's wedding and so it was sort of incumbent on my mother to take a particular interest in the fact that her oldest sister's oldest son still cut such a tragic bachelor figure.

I tried to lighten the atmosphere. 'Well, we certainly tried *our* best to get Manichettan married off, didn't we, Baluchetta?' I giggled at my brother, although the grown-ups didn't know what I was talking about.

I was referring to the time we had conducted a mock wedding during one of our lazier summer holidays. Manichettan was obviously the bridegroom and, because she was sweet and pretty, Devichechi was the bride. Manichettan's younger brother, Vinoochettan – even back then a portly character who had gone on to become a replica of his father – was the head priest while my brother, Baluchettan, younger by six months, was relegated to Assistant Namboothiri. The rest were assorted Family Members and, in the manner of those Greek tragedies that Nalinichechi seemed to know all about, the smallest of us were just a motley crew called Crowd. That certainly didn't stop us from bringing our utmost to our performance. It was a perfect wedding; the groom was handsome, the bride correctly bashful, the *podava* ('borrowed' from my mother's vast collection of silk saris) gratefully received. The father of the bride put up a convincingly tearful performance during the *kanyadaan*, nearly hijacking the denouement, but once his part was done, the Crowd launched into the most enthusiastic *korava*, ululating so loudly that the caterwauling brought Ammumma and the maids running outside in a panic to see what the commotion was about. When she saw that it was only Manichettan and Devichechi's 'wedding', Ammumma grinned. She was always a sport about all the stuff we got up to; yet being also deeply superstitious, I heard her mutter something about hoping this did not take away from both Mani's and Devi's *yogam* of getting married properly someday. I don't think she meant them getting married to each other even though, a mere eight, I already knew that the children of a brother and sister could technically get married to each other ('*mora*', they called the practice). However I occasionally harked back to that incident mostly because, by some weird coincidence, Devichechi had so far remained unmarried too. Not that it should be so unusual for a thirty-year-old medic in America to have not found the time yet for marriage and all its attendant responsibilities, but until either Manichettan or Devichechi got hitched, there was a part of me that was superstitious enough to retain a small element of Ammumma's concern voiced that day.

Valliamma's excitement, therefore, on finding out that my new company was sending me on a trainee scheme to Singapore was mixed in with one big vested interest.

'I am so *happy* you are going to Singapore, *moley*. At least you will be able to meet Mani and ask him why he has not replied to my letter about that girl in Kuwait. I even sent a photo. *Nice* girl, just a little bit on the plumpy side,' she said on the telephone.

'*Tcheh*, Valliamma, I'm not sure he'll want me interfering in all that,' I protested.

'Interfering? It is not interfering when a younger sister asks why her brother is not agreeing to marriage!'

'But marriage and all those kinds of things – they are too personal for everyone to take an interest, Valliamma. Especially me ... A younger cousin and all ...'

'Personal? Let me tell you marriage is the least personal thing amongst us, *moley*!' she admonished, adding in what I thought was sinister fashion, 'You wait, your turn is coming up soon also.'

She was referring, of course, to the fact that my brother Baluchettan had succumbed two years ago, marrying a 'nice' Malayali girl whom a relative of my father's had met in Delhi. The pair had been put in touch by email and, in the more modern manner of girl-viewing ceremonies, decided to meet in the coffeeshop of a five-star hotel when Baluchettan had a business meeting in the capital. He had insisted that there be no elders present and, despite a few mutterings from the likes of Gopumama down in Palghat, my parents had insisted that we were all progressive enough now to cope with these trends in Nair modernity.

Our Facebook cousins' page had buzzed for a few days with the excitement of Baluchettan having been bowled over at first sight, much amusement being garnered at the speed with which he had subsequently said yes. His enthusiasm had even taken my parents by surprise although I suspected that, mixed in with Amma's sheepishness that her son had overtaken four older cousins to the marriage post, was a small element of competitive pride. A *Malayali* girl too.

Manichettan had not been able to come to Guruvayoor for the wedding because it was a very busy time at his work place in Singapore; but he managed to make a two-day dash to Chennai where my parents hosted a reception the week after Baluchettan's wedding. I had not seen Manichettan for six years at that point. As this was his first visit back from Singapore, he hadn't changed that much and his was still a delightful presence to have around – the picture of tranquillity in the midst of a noisy family gathering, totally dignified even when he was being thrust before various girls and their eager parents along with the words, 'Engineer', 'Big Shipping Company', 'In Singapore'. But he had escaped that time too, his single status intact.

When I emailed him to say I was coming to his city, Manichettan's response was typically swift and sweet:

'So delighted you are coming to my town, little sis. In fact, you will be the first of my cousins to come and see me here, imagine that! But why only three days? I can't wait to show you around this great place and, since you have work too, that will leave barely any time. And what about all those hawker centres I told you about? Remember? You will just love the food they serve (you with your carnivorous tastes) and how many will we be able to eat at, given only three nights? And don't say you will have company dinners in the middle of that too. Please check all this and get back to me asap so that we can make proper plans. I am looking forward very much to seeing you soon. Love to you and Kunyamma-Kunyachen when you next speak to them, yrs, Manichettan.'

My company was booking all trainees into a fancy hotel on Orchard Road and also organizing a guided tour around Singapore and Sentosa. When the official programme was emailed to us, I also saw that, just as Manichettan had predicted, there were two evening engagements as well. That left only one evening 'free for shopping and personal visits', as the schedule said, and so I wrote again to Manichettan to ensure he would keep himself free for me that night.

'I think I might even be able to get away from my hotel so am happy to come across to your house,' I offered, feeling more and more thrilled.

'Can you not stay an extra day or two? Take leave?' came his reply.

'I think leave would be out of the question so early into my career, Manichetta! Sure you understand how it is with a new job and all?'

And, of course, he did. There were no more pleas, nor complaints. Instead Manichettan promised that he would keep free the evening that suited me. He would also come to the convention hall where the training session was due to take place and we would go straight from there for a 'great hawker-centre feast' as he put it.

Singapore was exactly as I'd imagined: smart, streamlined, beautifully behaved. A very civilised 'Manichettan' kind of place, in fact. From the car window, I watched polite, disciplined traffic negotiate the grid system as we drove into the city from Changi Airport and felt no surprise at how easily Manichettan had taken to life in this city. I recall he had even said, on the night of Baluchettan's reception (unusually dramatically for him), that he would be perfectly happy to die in Singapore and I could now see what he meant. If the city impressed me with all my demanding, big-city ways, then for someone with Manichettan's gentle and considerate nature, it must have felt like a perfect fit.

My two days in Singapore passed in a whirl before the evening I was due to meet Manichettan rolled around. At the close of the final training session, I hurried out of the seminar room and into the lobby and there he was – just as he'd promised, at 'precisely 7 pm' – dear old Manichettan, looking not that different from the gangly pre-teen boy from my childhood, my first memory of him. Just slightly taller and thinner and with a tiny bit less of that springy hair that always grew straight up from his head. Engrossed in a copy of *The Straits Times*, he did not notice me until I was right before him, startling him with a huge yell.

'*Edo*, you frightened me,' he said, laughing as he got up to hug me so enthusiastically that he lifted me clear off my feet. We did not need to exchange too many pleasantries, or too much gossip (thanks to our respective garrulous mothers), and so we were soon setting off into the Singapore night to get ourselves a drink and dinner. The lights of cars and neon signs on the street were dazzling after the muted glow of the hotel and warm damp air brushed pleasantly across my face which was still cold from the powerful air-conditioning that had blasted though my seminar room all day. We walked down the road in the direction of the nearest MRT stop with me chattering and Manichettan listening, just like it had always been.

'So, where are we going, Manichetta?' I asked finally, now unable to contain my excitement at the thought of the culinary feast awaiting me.

'You tell me. Order anything you want to eat, and I can put it before you within one hour straight.'

I had researched Singaporean food well and knew I wanted to try both *bak chang*, which the Internet informed me were the city's famed stuffed and steamed dumplings, as well as the claypot dishes that one of my colleagues had raved about after her own traineeship here last year.

'The question is – will my tummy have room for both *bak*

chang and claypot pork? How big are the portions here?' I asked Manichettan.

He laughed. 'From what I remember of your capacity for *puttu-kadala* and *pazham-pori* three times a day, your stomach is no delicate organ, is it?'

I smacked his upper arm and grinned up at him. 'You can talk,' I retorted, 'Hollow Legs, Gopumama used to call you!'

'How is he, old Gopumama?' Manichettan asked, a small cloud passing over his features. Our maternal uncle had suffered a heart attack six months ago and now barely left his house.

'As well as can be expected. Just waiting for Devichechi to get married, I suppose. Must be a bit of a worry for him,' I replied.

'And from what I can see, Devi's enjoying herself far too much in Boston to even think about marriage!'

I nodded. We all knew about Greg, the American boyfriend Devichechi had acquired about a year ago. Us cousins, that is. We had kept Greg a well-guarded secret from all our Valliammas and Kunyammas with good reason. No point in upsetting delicate sensibilities until Devichechi was sure this was the real thing. There had already been a few false alarms from her.

'Okay, back to our evening plans,' Manichettan cut into my thoughts, 'Let's go to Newton Food Centre – it's not far – and then you can decide what you want to eat. It's good to have an idea before reaching there, though, because the array of choices on offer makes it all quite confusing.'

'Was that how you felt when you first came to Singapore, Manichetta?' I queried. 'It was the first time you'd lived outside Kerala.'

He paused for a minute before replying. 'Was I confused, you mean?' He thought some more, furrowing his forehead as he always did before saying anything important. 'Hmm ... Yes, it was all a bit confusing, to be honest. But not in a bad way. There were so many new things to take on board, so many new experiences. Once my head stopped spinning around, I started enjoying myself. And now I just love it.'

We had descended into the bowels of the MRT and hopped into the first train that appeared before us. Manichettan scanned the digital display above the door and nodded. 'So busy talking, I forgot to ensure we're going in the right direction!'

'Are we?'

'Yes. And it's just a stop away. We'll be at Newton in under ten minutes.'

Standing next to each other, we chatted about my job and the traineeship, Manichettan curious to know about the workings of a cosmetics giant.

'They're interested in the growing Indian market,' I explained. 'R&D are even developing a whole new range for brown skin. Imagine, no more grey-brown faces with white in the creases!'

By the time we had concluded that India's 'emerging

middle class' made for a better market in utilitarian products rather than luxuries, we had arrived at our stop. Emerging from the station, I asked, 'Drink first, Manichetta?'

He looked surprise, 'I didn't know you'd started drinking.' I looked for a rebuke in this statement but Manichettan's tone was typically mild.

'Well, you don't get through IIM without sampling most things life has on offer,' I laughed as we walked towards a nearby hotel and entered the bar.

With a pair of beer glasses sweating gently on the table before us, we took up our conversation again: mostly family news mixed in with the occasional sentimental reminiscence about our holidays back in Ammumma's *tharavaadu*. I couldn't help noticing how adroitly Manichettan kept turning the conversation away from his own life and interests. Of course, he had always focused on the welfare of other people and, as a child, I had always taken this as a sign of his total unselfishness but now, a bit more grown-up myself, I found myself slightly irked by Manichettan's insistence that we talk about everything and everyone else but himself.

I put my glass down after a long swig. 'Now, tell me more about *you*, Manichetta,' I said, my tone bordering on strident (beer tended to fill me up with a strange kind of swagger).

'Me?' he looked surprised and then vaguely uncomfortable.

'Yes, you. You never talk about yourself, you know, Manichetta.'

'What is there to talk about me? I must be one of the

most boring guys in Singapore,' he laughed.

'Our dashing oldest cousin boring? Never!' I took another swig. 'Besides, I promised Valliamma that I would come back with *proper* news about you.'

'Proper news! What is that?' Manichettan's eyes were twinkling again.

'You know, proper news – what your house is like, what your day is like. Whether you cook for yourself or have a pretty little Singaporean who does that for you. You *know*.'

'Pretty little Singaporean,' he chuckled. 'I wish!'

'No? Nobody?' I persisted.

But Manichettan's gaze met mine in his usual calm and steady fashion as he repeated, 'No. Nothing like you imagine at all. And, if a pretty little Singaporean ever did come along, I promise you that my cousins would be the first to find out. There's no hiding anything from you lot, is there?' He paused before adding, 'As for my flat – I did think of taking you there tonight and even cooking up a home-made meal – but it's quite far out in Jurong and then I thought it would be a shame if you didn't get to see the hawker centres I'd told you so much about ... I said, didn't I, that time would be too short if you didn't extend your trip.'

'You're right, Manichetta,' I cut in, suddenly sheepish. 'I should have stayed longer. And that stuff about pretty Singaporeans – I'm only joking, you know that, don't you? But Valliamma is definitely going to quiz me when I get back!'

His laughter was affectionate but, again, I thought I saw

a small pensive shadow pass across his face. 'Poor Amma,' he said softly. 'Like with Gopumama and Devi, I sometimes think that Amma too will only really be at peace once I settle down and get married and have children. You think I should succumb just for her sake?' He asked the question lightly but I could not be sure he wasn't being serious.

'You say 'succumb' as though it's a battle!' I laughed, adding more gently, 'I guess Valliamma finds it hard when one of the younger cousins overtakes you,' I said.

'And there's been a few of those now!' He gave me a stern look. 'As long as *you* don't plan to overtake me too – now that would be the biggest blow!'

We laughed together and I was glad that the awkward moment had passed. I really had not intended to make Manichettan feel uncomfortable and cursed the beer for making me so thoughtless. I watched my beloved cousin now as he got up to take a call, walking away a few steps so as not to be talking into my face. Typical Manichettan, I thought, half listening to his end of the conversation in which I heard him ask his caller about the possibility of getting *bak chang* in the evening hours.

He sat down again at the table and asked, 'Hey, *moley*, would you mind if a friend joined us at Newton for dinner?'

'Not at all. Who is it? Could it be that I will at last meet that pretty little Singaporean?' I cried.

Manichettan grinned. 'Well, if you can call a six-foot bearded chemical engineer 'pretty' or 'little',' he retorted.

'Hey, now, six-foot engineer sounds good!' I chirped before suddenly sobering up and turning suspicious. 'This is not a set-up between you and *my* Amma, by any chance is it, Manichetta?'

'Set-up?'

'You know, "When she is there in Singapore, please introduce her to some nice Malayali boys whom you know etc., etc." Amma's starting to pile on the pressure onto me too ever since I graduated from IIM. Funny thing is she thinks she's being really subtle talking about "nice" boys all the time.'

Manichettan threw his head back and roared with laughter but I scowled, still feeling a little wary. It was certainly a bit weird that Manichettan had invited someone else to join us on our one evening together in Singapore. I persisted. '*Is* he Mallu, this bearded man joining us?'

'Aha, why don't you wait and see,' was Manichettan's rather frustrating reply.

We finished our beers and walked out into the balmy night again. Newton Food Centre, just two roads away, was throbbing with noise and light and steam was rising into the night air from the hundreds of woks that were being employed to toss food over burners. I could see cooks expertly throwing meats and sauces into noodles and vegetables and, surrounding them were hundreds and hundreds of diners, seated on narrow benches and tucking with great concentration into enormous bowls of food before them. The whole atmosphere was awash with the most delicious aromas.

'I've never seen anything like this before, Manichetta,' I breathed in awe.

Manichettan was already cutting his way past the diners on their benches. 'Come, let's find somewhere to sit. There's a guy on the far side who does the best claypot pork, I've found out.'

'From the six-foot beardy Mallu?' I couldn't help asking as I followed.

'That's it. Kit. Mallu as they come.'

Kit was already at the stall when we arrived, picking at a small bowl of *kimchi* with a pair of chopsticks, his computer case and a file being used to save the two seats across from him for us. We shook hands and I saw to my relief that this was certainly no Mallu being lined up for me. Nor, quite definitely, was he Manichettan's pretty little Singaporean but a burly Canadian, gruff of voice and gentle of manner. He was nice. And I could see what good friends he and Manichettan were, their easy camaraderie and conversation drawing me into what felt like a warm and welcoming and intensely private cocoon. I watched them choose the menu together and, when our food came, I noticed how they quietly anticipated each other's needs while making sure I was given the choicest bits, of course.

It was close to midnight by the time our extensive meal was over and we followed it up with something called *popiah* from a man apparently more famous for being surly than for his food. Then we went on to a stall to sample a dessert called *cheng tng*. When all that was done, Kit and Manichettan accompanied me back to my hotel and, after I had kissed them both goodbye, I stood for a few minutes on the steps, watching them head back to their flat in Jurong.

I ought to have been all puffed up that Manichettan had given me such a generous and trusting glimpse into his life, a far bigger deal than showing me his flat and giving me all the details of his job. Had he deliberately picked me of all the cousins to reveal this aspect to: his life in Singapore and this new kind of happiness he had found? But, as I turned to walk into the hotel lobby, it was a strange kind of fear that I felt, fluttering somewhere deep inside my stomach. Stepping into the lift, I thought of the number of times I had grandly predicted that Manichettan would die before making his parents unhappy. It was truly no exaggeration that he would far rather invite anguish on himself than see pain in his mother's eyes. That was just the kind of person he was. Did he now expect me to go back to our family in India and smooth his path for him in some way? I felt renewed panic; it was *he* who had always had that kind of clout with our elders, not me! I thought of how hard it would be to take up Manichettan's case, of the tears that would flow and the noisy recriminations that would follow. Would it be best to merely stay silent – as Manichettan himself had done all these years – so that he could cling to the happiness he had found for as long as he possibly could?

Jaishree Misra grew up between Delhi and Kerala and moved to England in 1990, when she was awarded a Charles Wallace for India scholarship to pursue a post-graduate diploma in Special Education at the University of London. Following this, she worked in the child protection services of Buckinghamshire County Council, as a radio journalist at the BBC and, most recently, as a film examiner at the British Board of Film Classification in London.

Jaishree has written seven novels, published by Penguin and Harper Collins, all of which have been Indian bestsellers. Her most recent book deal, with Harper Collins in the UK, was to write three commercial fiction novels. *Secrets & Lies*, published in July 2009, appeared soon after its release in the Heatseekers list of the UK charts. *Secrets & Sins* was released in August 2010 and *A Scandalous Secret* in July 2011. She has taken part in literary festivals at Jaipur, Hay-on-Wye, Hay Trivandrum, Kovalam, Mumbai, Hyderabad and Johannesburg and has participated at book fairs in Frankfurt, London and Sharjah.

Jaishree has an MA in English Literature from Kerala University and two post-graduate diplomas from the University of London, one in Special Education and the other in Broadcast Journalism. She recently moved back to New Delhi, where she is continuing to write alongside helping to develop a large integrated residential community for people with disabilities. Learn more at: *www.jaishreemisra.com*.

Patchwork

O Thiam Chin

It was May Lee's idea to get the patchwork blanket from her aunt, and to put it up on the wall in the bedroom in their new flat. The wait for the flat had been long, three years in fact, and now that they were in the final stages of decorating their home, May Lee wanted to put up something special, a personal touch, like a family heirloom or display, to bring everything into perfection, now that she and Peter were almost ready to begin their new life together. Then she remembered the call from Aunt Cheung, her late mother's younger sister, some months back, reminding her to collect the blanket from her. It had been passed down, through the generations, by the women of the family, and now it was May Lee's turn to take hold of it. She couldn't remember what it looked like, the colours or the fabric, but she wanted it – it would be the perfect thing for their new place.

'What's her address again?' Peter asked, wiping the perspiration off his forehead.

'We're almost there,' May Lee said, flustered by the heat and Peter's repeated questions. She checked the paper on which she had scribbled down the address. The words had turned smudgy. She looked around her, searching for the

O THIAM CHIN

landmarks that were not there anymore.

'Let me see, give me the paper.'

Peter stepped into the void deck of a block of flats, letting out a sigh of relief, glanced at the paper, and looked up to search for a road sign on the nearby street. May Lee walked away, looking out into the haphazard rows of ageing flats. It was an old estate, Ang Mo Kio, built during the time when the government was anxious about putting its growing population into adequate housing in the seventies. Now things had changed, and only old folks and poor families lived here. May Lee thought it was depressing how Aunt Cheung had lived the better part of her life here, alone, after her husband passed away more than ten years before.

'I don't understand why she doesn't want to move out of this place,' she said aloud. Peter looked up, tightened his face. He crumpled the piece of paper. 'She will die alone, and nobody will know.'

'It's her choice,' Peter said. 'You can't make her leave if she doesn't want to.'

A motorcycle passed them on the street, trailing a loud screech. 'She's my aunt. I'm just worried about her,' May Lee said.

Aunt Cheung was seventy-four, and she had treated May Lee like her own daughter since she only had sons – four of them – none of whom she had chosen to stay with. They had asked, and she had refused every single time. She took a liking to Peter when May Lee brought him for a visit, and

116

often asked after him when they talked on the phone, once in five or six months.

'We should get her some food,' May Lee said. 'I don't think she eats out much.'

She didn't know what kind of food Aunt Cheung liked. Definitely not instant noodles, she said the MSG gave her a sore throat. Even at her age, she still cooked her own meals, a simple meal with dishes like stir-fried cabbage with garlic or water spinach with dried shrimps, with rice or porridge. She stayed away from meat, which cost more, and she didn't think it was healthy to eat too much of it. Maybe she should get her some packets of salt or sugar, at least she could use them. And a large sack of rice, ten kilogrammes, she would need it too. May Lee tried to think of other essential things to get.

'Your aunt is a hardy person, she'll get by with anything,' Peter said. 'Let's go, I know where her block is.'

They walked in silence for another three blocks, crossing an open field with a dilapidated playground where two boys were playing on the grainy sand, burning something in a small dug-out hole. May Lee caught an acrid smell, like plastic burning, and glared at the boys; one of them scowled at her and challenged her stare. She turned away, disgusted. Her skin had reddened, breaking out in pinkish patches over her exposed arms and neck, and she regretted not wearing any sun block or a long-sleeved shirt. Unlike her, Peter tanned evenly under the sun, a man suitable for outdoor labour, and the tan gave him a sporty, weathered appearance.

They got to the block of flats, and at the void deck there was a handful of old men, gathering around a concrete table, smoking and chatting in different dialects. They took turns to spit on the floor, which was smeared with dark stains and wet spots. All of them looked at the couple with glassy reptilian eyes, expressionless. May Lee deciphered the dialects they were speaking and could identify three of them, and wondered how they could understand one another. Maybe they couldn't, and were just there for the companionship, she thought. The Indian *mamak* shop at a corner of the block was closed so they couldn't get what they wanted to buy for Aunt Cheung, and it seemed too troublesome to find another provision shop somewhere else.

They took the lift up to the tenth floor, and had to find their way along a dark corridor that seemed like a long airless tunnel with lights only at two opposite ends. They were careful not to trip over or knock down any pot of plants, or stray furniture, or overflowing prayer urns that were placed outside each flat unit.

Peter checked the unit number on the door and rapped twice. They waited, and hearing nothing from behind the closed door, May Lee leaned in to knock, harder and in quick succession. She was keenly aware of the noise, echoing down the quiet corridor and disturbing the other residents. Then a faint sound came towards the door. 'Please be nice,' May Lee said.

'I'm always nice,' Peter said, putting his hands into the front pockets of his trousers.

A head popped into view, and May Lee was taken aback as she saw the long gash on Aunt Cheung's right eyebrow and her sallow face which had hollowed out, giving her a ridge of protruding cheekbones. Her eyes, deeply creased at the sides, were milky but watchful.

'Oh my ...' May Lee said, stunned, unable to finish her words.

Aunt Cheung took some time to check their faces before finally recognizing them, and opened the front door. She smiled weakly, moved into the kitchen, and brought out two rickety stools. She wiped the surfaces with her hands, and gestured for them to sit. The stools were unbalanced, with the legs bending slightly inward.

'I'm so terribly sorry about the mess,' she said, and picked up a few loose pieces of clothing from a side table and balled them into a bundle. May Lee scanned the room, and shifted her body on the stool to balance herself. 'What happened?' she asked. Her tone came out wrong, almost accusatory.

'I was trying to clean the kitchen cabinets and wanted to take out the plates from the top shelf. But I wasn't tall enough so I had to use one of these stools. I barely stood on it, and the whole thing gave way.' She brought her fingers to the ribbed scar on her face, pulling back her shirtsleeve, and revealed a large peninsular of darkish-red, angry-looking bruises on her arms.

'They look quite bad, these bruises,' May Lee said.

'They are better now. It was much worse last week,' she said. 'Thankfully somebody found me, or I would have died.'

'Oh, Aunt Cheung.' May Lee wanted give her something, something that would bring quick relief, a bottle of ointment, or a tube of medicinal rub. She flinched at the thought that her aunt might have died if nobody found her, her body decomposing in the flat. That was how she had found her mother's body, in her bedroom, dead from a heart attack. She saw a frown on Peter's face. Her fears were confirmed, and she felt a stab of guilt. Her aunt was becoming helpless.

'Don't worry about me. I'm still as strong as a bull. If I didn't die this time, nothing can touch me,' she said, looking at May Lee, before lowering her eyes. May Lee got up, and the stool fell over nosily. Her aunt reached for the stool to put it upright again.

'You can't live alone now. It's not safe anymore,' May Lee said.

'What's not safe? It's just an accident,' her aunt said, tidying up the side table, distracting herself with the chore. 'This kind of thing happens all the time. There's nothing to worry about.'

'It's better to have someone keep an eye on you,' May Lee said. 'Just in case.'

'Don't worry, this only happened once. I'm more careful now.' Aunt Cheung picked up an empty plastic bag and swept a tiny pile of rubbish into it with her hand, ignoring the looks on the couple's faces. 'There are social workers who come around sometimes.'

May Lee wondered whether the social workers were the first ones to find her after the fall. Aunt Cheung read her mind, and said, 'No, it was the next-door neighbour, Mrs Wong. She heard the sounds.' May Lee exchanged glances with Peter, and said, 'Lucky thing she heard it. I can't imagine what would have happened.'

Her aunt left the room without replying. She came back with two glasses of water and put them in their hands. 'We look out for each other here,' she said, retiring into the kitchen again.

May Lee turned to Peter and whispered, 'We should do something.' She felt useless. Then they heard her call out, 'Stay for lunch, I'll cook a simple meal. It'll just take a while, so stay.'

May Lee got up and went into the kitchen, and turned down the request. She didn't want to impose, plus her aunt wasn't in the condition to cook, she needed to rest. Aunt Cheung insisted, and had started measuring out small cups of rice grains, pouring them into the rice cooker container. May Lee had to place her hand on her aunt's arm, to bring her actions to a stop. Her aunt turned to her, chastised, like a child being disciplined. It was true what they said about old people: as they got older, they slowly regressed into children, living out their second childhood, with the attendant moods and behaviours. May Lee softened her voice.

'Aunt Cheung,' May Lee said, changing the topic as she recalled the purpose of her visit. 'We are actually here to collect the blanket, the patchwork blanket. You called me to collect it from you.' She gave a searching look, then remembered. 'Yes, the blanket, I kept it for you. Let me look for it,' she said, wiping her hands on a piece of rag tied to the edge of the cooking stove. The rag was discoloured and dirty. May Lee followed her aunt back to the living room.

'Let me see where I've put it,' Aunt Cheung said, moving away a stack of newspaper on top of a storage carton box. 'It should be somewhere inside here.' May Lee noticed the contents of the box, filled to the brim with old clothes, and small tightly-bundled packages wrapped with yellowing newspapers. Aunt Cheung put aside some of these small packages on the floor, half-emptying the box. Peter stood up, and was looking at the framed portraits and old photographs on the wall, examining them, largely ignoring the two women. In one of the sepia photographs was a group shot, of four girls and three boys, lined up from the shortest to the tallest, standing before a single-storey kampong house, and he was trying to identify May Lee's late mother and Aunt Cheung. He was surprised at how the two women had closely resembled each other in their youth. He turned to look at the old woman now, bent with age and frailty, with a large newspaper-wrapped bundle in her hands. He continued his inspection of the other photographs.

'Do you still remember what it looks like?' Aunt Cheung

asked. 'Did your mother show it to you?' May Lee shook her head, smiling. The old lady unwrapped the newspaper carefully, peeling off the layers, afraid of damaging it. She lifted the blanket to May Lee. 'It's still quite good. Touch it, feel the fabric.'

May Lee ran her fingers across the surface of the blanket, which was made up of several different patches, each one of a different material, texture and colour. Chiffon, lace, sequins, organza, embroidery. It was a thick blanket, neatly folded, and parts of the edges were already fraying. She wondered how many pairs of hands the blanket had passed through to come to its present condition, to land in Aunt Cheung's possession. 'It's a beautiful blanket,' she said.

'Give me a hand, help me unfold it. I'll show you the whole thing,' Aunt Cheung said. May Lee held the corners and moved backward, spreading out the blanket. More colours and fabrics were revealed, each square of fabric connected to another, each a self-contained world of familial history. It was, in May Lee's estimate, two by two metres. She was stunned by its size, the sheer expanse of all that was expressed on it. She grasped it tightly, not wanting any part of it to touch the dirty floor.

'Your mother made the patch over there,' Aunt Cheung said, pointing to a spot on the blanket, near May Lee's hand. 'And I added the patch next to it. I cut out a piece from my old cheongsam, the one I wore for my wedding.' May Lee examined the two patches, one made of red chiffon and the other of latticed white silk, sewed together with a black thread onto an overall woollen fabric.

Aunt Cheung said, 'This blanket has been in our family for a long time, passed down from my mother to us, from her mother to her. And now it's yours.'

'How old is it?' May Lee asked, curious.

'I don't know, but my mother told me it's been passed down the family for many generations, even before her time, from woman to woman. Once you have it, you are supposed to add a piece of fabric to it, a part of you, your history, and then you hold onto it for a while, till you pass it to the next generation when it's the right time. Your mother wanted to pass it to you when it was your turn.' She smoothed out the crinkles in the blanket with a sweep of her bruised arm. 'But she didn't get the chance, because of the heart attack. She would have loved to pass this on to you.'

May Lee searched her mind for the past memories of her mother, of her talk about the blanket, but the images that were conjured up were sketchy, insubstantial. Only the very recent memories, of her sudden death and her funeral, were clear recollections, the rest was buried in the sands of time, entombed. 'My mother never mentioned this blanket to me at all,' she said.

'She must have. Or maybe you have forgotten.'

May Lee nodded, deferring to her aunt.

'Your mother and I used to spend a lot of time together looking at the blanket when we were young,' Aunt Cheung said. 'Back then we used it every night, to cover ourselves when it was cold. My mother, your late grandmother, believed that everything should have a use, and be put to use. She was practical in everyday things.'

She began to fold the blanket, and May Lee followed her rhythm so that the corners met and the blanket was folded up into a thick stack.

'We used to tell each other stories about the blanket, taking turn to feel each patch, and coming up with a new story. Our younger sisters joined in too. We came up with so many stories of heroines and swordsmen, of wolf-girls and hunters. There were sixteen patches then, including our mother's, so we never ran out of ideas or stories.'

May Lee put the blanket on her lap, her hands on it, rubbing the topmost fabric, made of a threadbare yellow silk. Her mother had told her once that one of the younger sisters had died of polio, and the other of malaria, because the family didn't have any money to treat them.

'Do you still want to keep it, for memory's sake?' May Lee said.

Aunt Cheung sat on a heap of old clothes tied up with nylon string. 'I have kept it long enough. I have added my patch,' she said, and looked at Peter who was still inspecting the old photographs on the wall. She put the blanket into a large pink plastic bag.

'You know the material your mother used for her patch? She cut out a part of an old dress that your father got her after they were married. She said it didn't fit her anymore after she had you.' Aunt Cheung smiled, baring a set of dentures. 'Take it, it's yours.'

'I don't know whether I should have it,' May Lee said, having second thoughts about the patchwork blanket, now aware of its history. She didn't know whether it was a good idea to display it anymore. 'I don't think I'll take good care of it.'

'Just take it out to air once in a while if you are not using it.' Aunt Cheung traced an embroidered pattern on one of the fabric patches, looking at the blanket. 'Remember the mothballs too.'

May Lee didn't want to put up any more resistance, realizing that the matter had been decided, long before she was born. 'Then I'll try my best to take care of it,' she said, getting up to leave. She called out to Peter, and he joined them at the front door.

'We'll come and visit you soon when we're free,' May Lee said, holding the plastic bag containing the patchwork blanket. She looked at her aunt's face, the scar, and was stricken by a sudden fear, of impending loss, of death. Aunt Cheung was at an age where everything was just a matter of time.

'When our place is done up, you can come and take a look.'

'Yes, I will,' Aunt Cheung said. She turned to Peter and held his hands. 'Don't forget to drop by anytime, you hear?'

'Yes, we will, we'll come by more often,' he said and put on his shoes at the door, not looking at her. Of course they wouldn't come again, at least not for a long while, but Aunt Cheung understood and forgave them and gave a benevolent smile.

'Next time I see you, bring along the blanket,' she said. 'Don't forget it.'

'I won't. I'll bring it along,' May Lee replied. They waited until Aunt Cheung had closed the door to begin walking away, down the dark corridor. Behind one of the flat units they heard someone coughing in a fury, and then sigh audibly. May Lee stopped in her tracks, the bag a burden in her hand. She finally had the blanket, the perfect piece of personal artefact to complete the home decor of their new flat, and now she had her doubts.

'Why, what's wrong?' Peter asked, looking back at her.

'Nothing's wrong, everything's good,' she said, gripping the handle of the bag, and joined Peter by his side. He took her hand, and took over the heavy bag. In the lift, he asked her, 'This is what you want, right? This blanket? The patchwork looks quite good.'

May Lee said nothing.

'Do you still want to frame it up? Think we need to trim it a bit, and custom-make a frame to hold it,' he said.

'Yes, we should frame it up. It'll look nice,' she said. 'It'll be the right thing to do.'

*   *   *

In the end, they put away the patchwork blanket in the storeroom, and put up a landscape portrait taken by a photographer friend, of a tribal village in China overlooking a rocky mountainous range, backlit by a dusky, dying sun. Everyone who saw it loved the portrait and praised the couple for their good taste, and May Lee was glad that she had made the right decision. Over time, she forgot about the blanket, and her own patch of fabric. Then a few years later, after Peter got a job promotion and a pay raise, and they decided to upgrade to an executive condominium in a better estate, May Lee discovered the patchwork blanket in the same plastic bag, pock-marked with cockroach-eaten holes, tucked in a corner of the storeroom when she was clearing out the old flat. She took a long look at it, put it into a box together with the other recyclables, and brought it down to the void deck where the recycling bins were. She left it there, among other people's broken, abandoned possessions, turned her back and walked away, already the memory of the patchwork blanket slipping away from her mind.

O Thiam Chin's short stories have appeared in anthologies: *ONE: Short Stories from Singapore's Best Authors*, *A Rainbow Feast: New Asian Short Stories*, *Malaysian Tales*; and literary journals: *World Literature Today*, *The International Literary Quarterly*, *Asia Literary Review*, *QLRS*, *Cha: An Asian Literary Journal*, *Kyoto Journal* and *The Jakarta Post*. He is the author of four story collections: *Free-Falling Man*, *Never Been Better* (longlisted for the Frank O' Connor Short Story Award), *Under the Sun* and *The Rest of Your Life and Everything that Comes With It*. He was an honorary fellow of the Iowa International Writing Program in 2010.

In Memory of Kaya Toast

Anjali Menon

I entered the room quietly. As I had done for the past two months, I poured tea into her china teacup. Next to the cup I placed the quarter plate, with a single toasted jam sandwich. I sat down beside her wheelchair under the roofed balcony. Like every day, she took a small bite of the sandwich and grimaced. Then, Ammumma turned around and looked at me, the first time ever since I had known her.

When I got engaged to Arun, he told me about his grandmother who lived with them. I caught a fleeting glimpse of her at the wedding. But it was only when I moved into Arun's parents' home in Kochi that I got to know her.

Every morning, Arun and his parents would leave for work and I spent my days in the company of the 87-year-old lady and a 17-year-old dog. My grandmother-in-law and the aging dachshund seemed to have a pact: to keep me at a distance. Not exactly the most inspiring company for a 24-year-old who was still in the honeymoon phase of her life!

Nevertheless I tried to please by doing small things

ANJALI MENON

like getting her tea served as she liked and where she liked. 'Chinese tea and jam toast sandwich, at 4 o'clock, in the balcony of her room that faces the garden downstairs.' All to see that grimace.

The tea was a brew of Chinese herbs. Arun credited it to 'the Far East hangover' that most of his family had from spending decades there. The jam toast sandwich seemed rather lowly company to the lofty tea. 'But that's how she likes it,' said my mom-in-law, rolling her eyes.

Age had lightened Ammumma's eyes but not her vision. She seemed to look into me, probing to see something of value. Something must have seemed right because she then showed me a postcard. On the front was a photo of the Singapore Merlion. Turning it over, I found it was addressed to Madame Rugmini Nair. Pretty orchid blossom stamps lined the upper edge and below that was a note in very neat handwriting. Someone called Tim wrote that his grandmother May Shue was visiting Kochi and she would call on Ammumma on 27th June.

When I looked up from the postcard, Ammumma's eyes were on me. 'Can you cook?'

For years my mother had been urging me to learn the skills of a homemaker to avoid embarrassment in a situation exactly like this. All in vain. 'Just some basic things.'

'Good. Those who know too much, cannot be taught.'

That night, when I gleefully phoned my mother to share Ammumma's grand opinion, she refused to believe it. She warned me that it could be the beginning of a real lesson for my past indolence. As I hung up I remembered Ammumma's last comment that morning: 'We don't have too much time.'

Whatever she was planning, a whole month lay between us and the said date. But perhaps at her age, a month or two was hardly any time.

The next day at tea time, after the grimace, she asked me to make a list which she dictated:

> *Kumbalappam* – steamed dumplings filled with
> jackfruit jam
> *Thayiirvada* – fried lentil patties dunked in sweet
> yoghurt
> *Idiappams* – string hoppers made of rice
> *Ishtoo* – a mild stew of meat & coconut milk
> Tea

'No jam sandwich?'

Her stern, raised eyebrow finished any doubts I had.

I was familiar with each of these dishes; they were all short eats served in homes in Kerala before the invasion of chips, Cheez Balls and the like. I had enjoyed endless portions of these in my grandma's home but had never seen them being cooked. Yet now I was on my way to purchase the ingredients to make them. I was to get the 'real ingredients', no short cuts allowed.

The *kumbalappams* required jackfruit but it was not the

season for the fat fruit. So after visiting a few shops I returned home with everything else.

'Jackfruit?'

The one word and smirk sent me scurrying back to the shops and known fruit vendors in town. But no luck – though the monsoon was delayed and it was still summer, the jackfruit trees weren't aware of this. Eventually our driver's aunt offered a jackfruit that grew in their garden. Apparently their tree always ran late in the annual flowering cycle. Thank the Lord!

As the housekeepers sorted the ingredients, Ammumma wheeled herself into the kitchen. Her loyal dachshund had been banished from the proceedings. Instructing the staff to place all the ingredients on the dining table, she turned to me: 'You do it.'

Her careful eyes watched me as I picked up each pack and emptied it into bottles and jars. Every spill resulted in a silent twitch that I began to dread. Ammumma wanted me to prepare all the ingredients and get them ready for use in the dishes. This involved sorting, sieving, grinding, roasting and storing.

My fingers flew through the pulses instead of a keyboard and my eyes keenly watched the textures emerge as we worked on them. I found my confidence dipping whenever Ammumma traced an imperfection in the process. She wouldn't say much but it was made clear that I had to start over.

With the jackfruit there wasn't such luxury because I knew how hard it had been to find this one. So I tried to be careful as I dissected the fruit. Each seed was removed and the soft ripe pulp was taken apart. Dark jaggery was melted in a huge brass vessel along with clarified butter, and into it went the golden pulp. The low heat fused their flavours, colours and textures over many hours of cajoling with a brass spatula. It was an arduous process that transformed the plain old jackfruit into a rich thick delicious preserve. Ammumma asked me to taste it before giving her a sample.

The sticky blob filled my mouth and mind with a rich sweetness that brought back memories of childhood vacations and temples where I had sensed this taste deeply immersed in milk desserts. When I opened my eyes I was actually thankful to Ammumma, for taking me back that far.

We got things ready for the other dishes on the menu but there was something special about the jackfruit jam. She asked me to pack a bottle of the jam for May Shue and keep it aside before filling the *kumbalappams*. This left me overjoyed as she obviously approved of how the jam turned out!

Despite all these discussions, Ammumma never mentioned the postcard or the impending visitor to any one else in the family. So I didn't either. Every evening before the others arrived, all the ingredients would be packed and put back in their place and Ammumma would be back in her balcony staring into space, the dachshund by her side.

One evening when everyone was at the dinner table,

Ammumma gently cleared her throat, 'May Shue is visiting next week.'

Everyone looked up but only my mom-in-law recognized the name: 'May Shue ... from Singapore days? Oh my ... How did she contact you?'

Ammumma, in her characteristic way, didn't bother to reply. So I piped in: 'Her grandson sent a postcard.'

'Oh my god! Tiny Tim is coming too?'

That was enough to send my mom-in-law reeling into her childhood memories of Singapore in which May Shue seemed to play an integral role. She explained that May Shue made the best *avial* in the Far East, thanks to Ammumma's recipes.

The morning of 27 June when I came down the stairs, Ammumma was showered and dressed in the gold-bordered *veshti mundu* that I had laid out the previous night. She had been through her usual routine of medicated oil massage, a hot bath with neem leaves, and a generous dousing of talcum powder. I noticed that the bottle of cologne on her dresser had moved a bit too. As she sat on her wheelchair in the balcony, Ammumma looked every bit the proud princess she was named after.

Though the postcard didn't say anything, Ammumma was sure that May Shue would visit at teatime. So after lunch she chose the crockery and the napkins that we would use. From a rather large collection of napkins with Chinese embroidery, she chose a set of white silk napkins with pale blue butterflies.

We had done a trial run of all the dishes. So I felt more confident about making them this time around. The dumplings were steamed to a plump luminous texture and Ammumma was almost smiling in approval when the doorbell rang. Suddenly I saw her expression change – Madame Rugmini Nair was nervous. She turned to me, 'I want to answer the door.'

I leaned over Ammumma's wheelchair and the dachshund to open the door. There stood a smiling man in his thirties; from behind him peeked a small old woman. She wore pale trousers and a t-shirt with a scarf around her head. When she saw Ammumma, her wizened face crinkled into a wide smile. Ammumma held out her arms and they embraced. All four of us stood cramped at the threshold until I spoke, 'Shall we go inside?'

They sat next to each other holding hands for a long time, but there was no conversation. I didn't know what to do. So I headed off to prepare the dining table. Once everything was laid out exactly as instructed, I went back to find them exactly the same way. I asked, 'Shall we have some tea?'

Tim smiled and stood up. May Shue suddenly muttered something to him in Chinese. He looked into her large handbag and pulled out three glass jars. Tim handed them to me: 'When Granny worked in Madame's kitchen, she would serve her kaya toast, made with the local coconut jam. Madame used to like it then. So she made some kaya before we started for India.'

When he handed me the bottles, Ammumma turned to me. Quickly, I brought out our bottle of jackfruit jam and handed it over. May Shue was suddenly excited and she urged Tim to ask me something, 'Granny would like to know if this is the homemade Kerala jam that Madame told her about in Singapore?'

Before I could say anything, Ammumma nodded to her and said in Malayalam, '*Athu thenne. Ninakku vendi undaakichatha.* (It's the same one. It is made for you.)'

Tim and I were superfluous to the rest of the conversation as the ladies chatted away in their own languages and the dishes on the dining table remained untouched.

Ammumma asked for the tea to be brought into the balcony with only slices of fresh toast. The two jams were generously spread onto separate slices and the ladies sat back in their chairs with the dachshund between them. The only sound was of dentures gently chewing through sweet toast. And gentle raindrops.

Finally, the monsoon had come and the grimace was gone.

Anjali Menon is a filmmaker and writer who has lived more years as an immigrant outside India. She returned to her home country in 2003 and currently lives in Mumbai with her husband and son.

A Commerce graduate, Anjali Menon received her Masters in Communication Studies from Pune University in India. At the London International Film School, London UK, she acquired another Masters in the Art & Technique of Film-making (specialising in Writing & Direction); graduating with distinction honours in Film Editing, Film Producing & Film Direction. She has further trained at workshops held by Script Factory & Julian Freidmann.

Her fiction film writing, direction and editing work have received acclaim and travelled to over forty international film festivals. She has been the recipient of Best Screenplay, Best Director, Best Film awards including those instituted by FIPRESCI, British Film Institute and Mira Nair. Her writing reflects themes of immigrant experience, reverse migration, cross-generational relationships and social disparities.

Anjali Menon has founded Little Films India, a film company based in Mumbai that produces fiction and documentary films. In addition, she has addressed seminars and workshops about fiction film writing and served as a Jury member at the International Film Festival of Kerala. A trained classical dancer and an active blogger, Anjali Menon's writing can be read on *www.anjalimenon.com*. She is currently working on her first book of short stories in English.

Taste

Verena Tay

{ Dedicated to my siblings and nieces }

The moment he pushed his luggage cart through the terminal doors towards the passenger pick-up point, Martin finally knew he was back in Singapore. Though the sky was overcast like a grey London day, the steam bath humidity descending on him was definitely not London. Perspiring, he quickly stripped off his waistcoat sweater to preserve whatever crisp dignity in his white shirt that was left after the thirteen-hour flight.

'You okay?' queried his elder sister Marion.

'I'm fine. Just not used to the heat.'

Piped up Michie as she skipped behind the siblings, 'When were you last here, Uncle Mart?'

'Hmm … Must be eight years ago. When Ah Kong died.'

'When I was two! I was small.'

'Yes. Then, you were only this big. When you last visited me in London, you were this high. And now, you're already at my shoulder.'

'Soon, I'll be taller than you and Mummy! Yay!'

Marion took charge, 'Martin, I'll bring the car around. Michie, you want to stay or follow me?'

'Stay! Uncle Mart, where's Uncle George? Why didn't he come along with you?'

Martin felt his chest tighten.

'Mich!' warned Marion, shooting nervous eyes of apology to her brother.

'But Mum!' protested the innocent child.

Motioning that all was well, he urged his sister to continue towards her car and turned to his niece, 'We broke up, Michie.'

'Oh ... That's so sad!'

Michie flung her chubby arms around his waist and hugged him tight. Touched, he patted her on the head.

'Thanks, Michie. Everything's okay.'

Unwrapping herself from him, she said, 'I liked Uncle George.'

'So did I.'

'He was nice. He used to buy me yummy Swiss chocolates. He couldn't play Angry Birds though.'

'Really?'

'Yah, I always beat him. So what did you eat on the plane, Uncle Mart?'

Martin patiently listened to the little seasoned traveller prattle on comparing airline cuisines. For a brief moment he was glad to be in Singapore, if only to see how his niece had grown since her last London visit with her parents during the previous Christmas. As Michie chatted away, he gazed at her eyebrows and forehead and realised how the child was losing her soft roundness and gaining the angularity of the family cheekbones and forehead, once so prominent in her grandfather, his father. Then all his unease of flying back to the land of his birth returned.

Seeing the familiar countenance in Michie, he remembered when he had last gazed at Dad's brow a few days' before he suffered the stroke that killed him. It was at the first brunch of Martin's annual visit back to Singapore, the usual pilgrimage by father and son to the Maxwell Road Hawker Centre. Dad filled their table with orders of Martin's childhood favourites, such as *ham chin peng*, *char kway teow*, fish porridge, *bak kut teh*, *bak chor mee*, oyster pancake – dishes he had gleefully introduced to Martin decades earlier during their Sunday foodie explorations all over town. While watching Martin sample the buffet, Dad once again tried to persuade Martin to live and work in Singapore on a permanent basis, settle down, and raise a family. When Martin refused, Dad frowned, the furrows in his forehead creasing to their maximum. Then Dad sighed and muttered, 'Hah, no use! *Jiak kantang eh lang*!', shaking his head in disbelief at how all the delicious local fare in front could fail to seduce his son away from being a 'potato-eater' living in the West.

But Dad could never understand how the pull of London exerted a far greater force on Martin than the attraction of family and hawker food. As soon as National Service was over, Martin moved away from humid, uncool, conservative Singapore to construct the life he had always dreamed about in temperate, cosmopolitan, glamorous and liberal London. He studied fashion design and slogged to make his mark in the international arena. He met and lived openly with George, an Englishman ten years his senior, sharing a spacious apartment in Hampstead. Dad's sudden passing finally freed Martin from his filial responsibilities and allowed him to live wholeheartedly in London. He could forget about Singapore, except for the occasional call or email from Marion and her yearly visits to the British capital with her husband and Michie.

And Martin was happy. Until five months ago.

After a long day troubleshooting for his autumn showcase of women's accessories, he arrived to an empty home and a Post-It from George on the fridge that scrawled: 'Moved to Ibiza with Som. The apartment is yours. Bye and take care.' To be so casually dumped after sixteen years in favour of a Thai toy boy of twenty that George met not too long ago, Martin was devastated. He tried his best to cope. During the day, he could go to his office or work out at the gym and forget everything else. The nights, however, were unbearable. Memories of life with George filled each room of the Hampstead flat. In particular, what Martin missed most were the hearty suppers that George the gourmet cook would rustle up on most evenings from exotic ingredients or mundane leftovers to welcome Martin home. These meals satisfied Martin's physical hunger and were warm preludes to the lovemaking that often came after.

So life without George meant no longer eating well, losing weight and crying to sleep alone on the art deco bed they had chosen together seemingly aeons ago. As time passed, Martin grew more depressed and confused as he began to question the choices he had made. Then Marion called, having found out about the spilt. She commanded: 'Come back to Singapore. Take a break. Spend Christmas with us, instead of moping in London.' Initially, Martin resisted, assuring her that he was fine and citing work pressure. She would not take no for an answer. She simply bought and emailed him a business class ticket for him to spend two weeks at her Ardmore Park home for the holidays. Martin was touched. Perhaps Marion was right: some family time might help. And despite his reservations about Singapore, perhaps a way forward beyond the present heartache was to go backwards for a short while.

Thus Martin found himself seated in Marion's Lexus on the expressway heading towards town, unable to stop marvelling at the slew of new condos, public housing flats and factories that lined the route. He remarked, 'All these developments – they weren't around before.'

'You know Singapore,' replied his sister. 'Boom or bust, business as usual: build, build, build.'

'What the ...'

Suddenly, heavy monsoon rain blanketed the car and all the buildings vanished. The storm that had been threatening to break for the last thirty minutes was finally descending.

'It's December,' Marion said, adjusting her driving speed, 'what do you expect?'

'So much so fast? I don't remember this kind of rain.'

'The weather's kind of crazy these days. Global warming, I guess. It's been pretty wet this season, pouring every day, and quite often like that.'

'Mummy,' Michie asked from the back seat, 'is Orchard Road going to flood again?'

'Maybe, Michie, who knows?' answered Marion before responding to her brother's quizzical look. 'There've been times when one month's worth of rain falls within two, three hours, causing flash floods everywhere, including Orchard.'

'Really?'

'Uh-huh,' affirmed Michie. 'Uncle Mart, have you got my Christmas present yet?'

'Why?'

'If you haven't, and if Orchard doesn't flood, can we go to Taka and then you can ...'

'Mich!'

'What?'

'Uncle Mart's just only arrived. Let him rest first and then decide. Remember, it's his holiday, not yours.'

'Okay.'

'If Michie wants to go to Taka, let's!'

'Yay!'

'Alright, tomorrow then. But surely you've other plans

for your visit, other than spoiling Michie?'

'Just catching up with you guys, really. And ...'

'What?' probed Marion.

'Local food, of course! Lots of it,' grinned Martin. 'It's still hard to get decent chicken rice in London. Is Maxwell still open?'

'Yup! Oh, but you can get hawker food anytime, anywhere. So many new, exciting joints that opened up in the last few years that I must bring you to,' enthused Marion. And for the rest of the car ride, she gushed about the culinary delights of Dempsey, Rochester and Marina Bay Sands, with eager contributions from Michie. Martin listened and let himself be enveloped by his family. Outside the car, the rain continued to fall.

* * *

Shielding himself as best as he could from the December downpour under the small, foldable umbrella he had borrowed from Marion, Martin dashed across the street towards the row of pre-war shophouses. By the time he reached the sheltered five-foot way, his deck shoes and gym bag were drenched. Yet he refused to let the dampness distract him during this day of self-exploration.

Marion had been a gracious hostess, chauffeuring him around to visit aging relatives, see the latest sights, shop for gifts, and test new eateries. Surrounded by family and a new environment, the hurt of the break-up with George was beginning to ease. However, the daily interaction with Marion and her family was getting a bit too much, especially for Martin's middle. Marion's idea of showing off the culinary best of Singapore was to visit top restaurants to gorge on set lunches, buffets and ten-course dinners. After five days of non-stop feasting, Martin was dying to work out and burn the extra calories. He also longed to actually walk the city streets and re-connect with Singapore face-to-face, instead of through the glass windows and comfort of his sister's Lexus.

So when Marion said her office was calling her back from her annual leave to take care of urgent business and that Michie had to attend some remedial Mandarin classes, Martin stated he would spend the day out by himself. After morning exercise at the downtown club that he had complimentary rights to use based on his London gym membership, he deliberately walked away from the central business district filled with its tall, glass-and-steel offices towards the older, humbler parts of town to see if he could still recognize the streets that he used to roam as a child holding onto Dad's hand.

He was rather disconcerted. Quite a few of the shophouses had been refurbished and converted into boutique offices for design firms and internet start-ups or even into neon-fronted pubs and bars. There was little left of the old-world charm that he remembered from his youth. Then as the sky darkened with impending rain again once more, he spotted in the distance a row of old, un-renovated buildings, their facades darkened by years of tropical mould and lichen that tend to grow profusely on painted exterior walls. Instinct told him to head that way when rain started pelting down.

On the five-foot way, he closed the umbrella and shook it, sending a spray of rain water cascading across the pavement. He glanced around. He was standing in front of a former tailor shop, recently closed, as indicated by the big sign taped to the shutters advising clients to seek the tailor at his new premises in a shopping centre. He could barely read the notice since there was no light from the shop and storm clouds blocked the sun. Gazing down the gloomy five-foot way, he realised that other shops were also permanently shut. Carefully, he made his way down the dark row. Of the few businesses that were open, he passed a Chinese medical practitioner-cum-dispensary, a hardware store, an importer of dried goods – all filled with ancient shopkeepers who lifted up their heads from their various tasks upon his approach, questioning the presence of a youthful stranger in their midst on such a wet day.

At the end of the block, he came upon a traditional *kopitiam* seemingly forgotten by time, its dull walls probably last painted thirty years ago. Pendant bulbs of low voltage hung from the ceiling, vainly lighting the dim interior. Dusty, wall-mounted fans swivelled from side to side, doing their best to shift the humid air. The surface of the marble-top tables were chipped, cracked or pitted. The wooden chairs were scuffed and scratched. A cockroach boldly marched across the grimy, mosaic-tiled floor, laying claim to its territory.

In spite of the squalor, Martin felt drawn to this old-style coffeehouse that reminded him of the places Dad used to bring him to years ago. There was a certain honesty that he liked about the *kopitiam*. It had no pretensions to be more than what it was, unlike the expensive restaurants Marion was fond of frequenting, the concept cafés now so common both in London and Singapore, or the plastic artificiality of modern, air-conditioned food courts that served generic fare prepared by disinterested cooks.

The two inhabitants of the *kopitiam* were just as down-to-earth and looked as if they had worked there for decades. A thin, leathery old man sat hunched over the front table facing the road with his right knee raised, his foot on the chair tucked beneath his bum. Wearing black flip-flops, khaki bermudas and a once-white undershirt, he stared balefully at the rain. Loudly, he grumbled to his companion seated behind him, '*Lok hor arh ni tam, bo lang lai! Aiyah! Arn chuah tarn?*' The woman, her white roots showing badly through permed, black-dyed hair, sniffed in reply to his complaint about the lack of business from the rain, checking the nasal drip caused by her diligent chopping of red chilies. Then she stopped her task, reached under the collar of her floral polyester top to remove her hankie that was tucked into her bra strap and used it to mop the sweat from her forehead.

In the end, what made Martin pause, enter the shop

and seat himself at one of the middle tables was not the old man's brusque invitation, '*Laoban, jiak xi mie?*' It was the aroma emanating from the simmering soup pot in the only functioning food stall situated at the front. The meaty caramel scent hinted at the expertise with which the essence of pig and prawn had been extracted and enhanced with an exact blend of condiments and spices, sure evidence that he was in the presence of a master chef who had honed his skills through years of preparing his one dish.

To pay homage to such craft, Martin ordered a large Hokkien prawn mee soup and a *kopi-o*. While the woman scurried to the rear of the shop to prepare the black coffee with sugar, the old man got up stiffly and shuffled in his slippers towards his stall. With mindless familiarity slowed by arthritis, the hawker blanched yellow noodles and green *kangkong* before laying them at the bottom of a bowl. Over the mee and vegetables, he placed a generous layer of par-boiled, medium-sized prawns, plus stewed pork ribs and pig skin. At last he ladled in the promising broth, garnished everything with fried shallots, and served the steaming bowl to his sole customer.

His coffee lay untouched while Martin tucked into the much anticipated *heh mee tng*. He was not disappointed. The prawns were succulent, the pork flesh melted away from bone and cartilage, the vegetables had a satisfying crunch, and the noodles were cooked to the right al dente consistency. Above all, the soup looked and tasted even better than it smelt. Not oily, the broth was dark brown, almost black, and packed with a dense texture that he had not encountered since he was of kindergarten age when Dad placed a Chinese-spoonful of similar soup at his lips and commanded, 'Try.'

He could not believe that anyone still prepared such flavour and body in the twenty-first century since he thought the art had died out long ago. The closest comparison he had in recent years was George's French onion soup, its combination of onions, beef broth, sherry, thyme and cheese never failing to cheer him on cold winter nights. Yet the old man's creation was far more powerful, nothing less than soul food. With each mouthful, a sense of warm well-being percolated further through his body, reviving the parts of him that had been shattered by the break-up and even awakening more forgotten memories of Dad lifting him onto high stools at roadside hawker stalls in Chinatown, his taste buds tantalised with first dishes and his belly filled with comfort.

Finishing every bit of the noodle soup and leaving only prawn shells and pork bones in the bowl, Martin sat back, enjoyed his coffee and welcomed the budding return of his old self. Only then was he again aware of his surroundings. Both the old lady and the hawker had returned to their former seats: she was peeling a pile of shallots and he was conversing with her in both Mandarin and Hokkien.

'Ah Tiong, damn lucky!' declared the old man.

'Really?' she grunted.

'Don't know how he got that Channel 8 star to come to

his *laksa* shop, take picture. Then he put the photo on the glass window. *Wah*, after that, business so good!'

'If you do the same, no use.'

'Sure or not?'

'*Aiyah*, got new people walk by this shop anymore and see your picture?'

The hawker motioned to Martin.

'This one special case,' she rebutted. 'The only people who usually come here are your regulars. This area is now dead. Better close up and retire!'

'How to retire? You got money, *mah*?'

She did not answer. A few seconds later, the old man exclaimed, 'I know!'

'Know what?'

'We must get young people to talk about our *kopitiam* on their computers and handphones!'

'You crazy or what?'

'Where got crazy? They carry these things everywhere. All the time, you see them press, press, press, play, play, play, talk, talk, talk …'

'You know people who want to do this for you, or not?'

'I buy and learn, *lah*!'

'You got money, *mah*? You so old, can or not?'

The hawker shut up. The old woman continued her work in silence.

Martin sat where he was, now feeling a little awkward. Outside the *kopitiam*, the rain petered to a light drizzle. It was time for him to leave. He stood up, asked to pay his tab and was amazed to learn from the coffee lady that his entire lunch cost about one-hundredth of the eight-course Chinese seafood dinner that Marion had splurged on the night before. In appreciation for what they had provided him, he faced the old man and said, '*Ah Chek, kam xia. Jin hoh chiak!*'

Responding to Martin's praise, the hawker broke into a wide smile, his previous sullenness broken, and replied, '*Hoh, hoh! Ow bai ko lai!*'

Not only did he promise he would return, Martin also said that he would bring his family to try the *kopitiam*. Pleased, the hawker and the coffee lady waved him goodbye as he walked away.

* * *

'Uncle Mart, are we there yet?'

'Almost, Michie.'

'Goodness, where on earth are you leading us to? The *heh mee tng* better be worth the 9.5 you rated it.'

'Absolutely, Marion! Tastes just like the old days, I guarantee!'

It had taken a week to convince Marion and Michie to brave the rain and travel outside their comfort zone, but Martin was finally fulfilling his promise to the old couple just two days before his return to London.

'Here we are!'

'Are you sure, Uncle Mart? It's closed!'

'Oh!'

The lights in the *kopitiam* were switched on as before to give illumination during the damp and dark morning. However, the prawn noodle soup stall was closed and the coffee lady was packing utensils and bowls into cardboard boxes. Upon their approach, the old woman called out, '*Heh mee tng boh liao!* Uncle *leh bai arh mi see kee. Sim zong.*'

Hearing that the hawker had died three nights ago of a heart attack, Martin was saddened. Suddenly, Singapore – and the world – was a little poorer.

For over 25 years, Verena Tay has acted, directed and written for local English-language theatre in Singapore, working for companies such as The Necessary Stage, ACTION Theatre, TheatreWorks and Practice Theatre. She created various solo and collaborative performances, often based on original, self-written material while she was as an Associate Artist with The Substation (2002–09). Her published collections of plays include: *In the Company of Women* (2004), *In the Company of Heroes* (2011) and *Victimology* (2011). She now focuses on writing fiction.

An Honorary Fellow at the International Writing Program, University of Iowa (Aug-Nov 2007), Verena teaches voice and presentation skills at various educational institutions and coaches people on how to improve their craft in storytelling and creative writing. She has also marketed books as well as edited publications on issues of teaching and learning in higher education.

For more information, please visit: *www.verenatay.com*.

Author Copyrights

About Insight India 2012

Insight India is an initiative envisioned by DFP Singapore. The initiative aims at bridging the gap between Tier 2 cities in India and global business hubs such as Singapore through cultural and business exchanges to actively foster collaboration, resulting in mutual benefit for both parties involved.

Insight India 2012 is a venture of literary and cultural exchanges undertaken to connect the city of Singapore with the upcoming Indian city of Trivandrum. It is supported by Dr Shashi Tharoor, Member of Parliament, Former Minister for State and Former Under-Secretary General for communications and Public Information (United Nations). Artists will collaborate to create a fusion of cultures displayed through an anthology of short stories (i.e. *A Monsoon Feast*), stage performances, collaborative sculptures and the development of exchange programs for students of the arts.

By building connections, *Insight India 2012* aims to facilitate stakeholders in Singapore and Trivandrum to form symbiotic relationships that aid in both cities moving forward while sharing their economic and cultural strengths in a supportive yet diverse environment.

About DFP

Founded in 2009 in Singapore, DFP is the brainchild of two professionals, Ms Payal Nayar and Ms Shalaka Ranadive, who have extensive experience in pioneering arts, cultural and business initiatives.

DFP, a high-end event management company, combines the creativity, marketing skills and event production experiences of its two directors to generate ventures for the service and media industries in Singapore. Apart from successfully integrating and promoting local Singaporean arts and cultural talent, the company has sponsored and facilitated cultural business exchanges by showcasing works of international artistes in Singapore. In addition, DFP has the expertise to set up and manage start-up companies as well as to handle training and education programs for schools and institutes.

One of DFP's key missions is *Insight India*, a sustainable project endeavouring to establish cultural and business ties between Singapore and emerging Tier 2 cities in India. The first city in India for this initiative is Trivandrum in Kerala. To contact DFP, please email payal@dragonflyproductions. asia and/or shalaka@dragonflyproductions.asia.

Acknowledgements

DFP would like to personally thank the following people and organisations that have made *A Monsoon Feast* possible:

- Dr Shashi Tharoor, for being so supportive and encouraging;
- National Arts Council (Singapore) for providing us the funding as well as a prestigious platform like The Singapore Writers Festival 2012 to launch the book;
- Professor Kirpal Singh and Dr Shashi Tharoor for writing the forewords;
- Monsoon Books for producing a wonderful book;
- Verena Tay, for working tirelessly to meet the deadline as the editor and contributor, and, more importantly, believing in us;

and, last but not least, all the other wonderful contributors, whose incredible stories have made *A Monsoon Feast* a very special book:

- Suchen Christine Lim;
- Dr Shashi Tharoor;
- Felix Cheong;
- Jaishree Misra;
- O Thiam Chin;
- Anjali Menon.

Special Thanks

DFP Singapore wishes to recognise the following contributors who have supported this book:

- Ambassador, Mr Gopinath Pillai, Executive Chairman of Savant Infocomm;
- Mr Vinod Menon, Chairman, Mindwave Solutions Pte Ltd;
- Mr Anil Thadani;
- Malayala Manorama;
- 'Kerala Tourism', the Tourism Organization of Kerala. Kerala, God's Own Country;
- Dr Gideon Hari Omm-Singapore.

God's Own Country

Official Websites of the Authors in

A Monsoon Feast

Suchen Christine Lim
www.suchenchristinelim.com

Shashi Tharoor
www.tharoor.in

Jaishree Misra
www.jaishreemisra.com

Anjali Menon
www.anjalimenon.com

Verena Tay
www.verenatay.com